HOWE·LIBRARY

HANOVER
NEW HAMPSHIRE

TROLLED

Favorites by
BRUCE COVILLE

AND DOZENS MORE!

The Enchanted Files

TROLLED

BRUCE COVILLE

illustrations by Paul Kidby

Random House New York

Text copyright © 2017 by Bruce Coville
Jacket art copyright © 2017 by Andrew Bannecker
Interior illustrations copyright © 2017 by Paul Kidby

All rights reserved. Published in the United States by Random House Children's Books, a division of Penguin Random House LLC, New York.

Random House and the colophon are registered trademarks of Penguin Random House LLC.

Visit us on the Web! randomhousekids.com

Educators and librarians, for a variety of teaching tools, visit us at RHTeachersLibrarians.com

Library of Congress Cataloging-in-Publication Data
Names: Coville, Bruce, author. | Kidby, Paul, illustrator.
Title: Trolled / Bruce Coville ; illustrations by Paul Kidby.
Description: First Edition. | New York : Random House, [2017] | Series: The enchanted files | Summary: Ned Thump is a seven-foot troll who is made fun of for his love of words so he escapes from the Enchanted Realm to the human world and secretly becomes a night watchman at Grand Central Terminal.
Identifiers: LCCN 2016015194 | ISBN 978-0-385-39259-4 (hardcover) | ISBN 978-0-385-39260-0 (hardcover library binding) | ISBN 978-0-385-39261-7 (ebook)
Subjects: | CYAC: Trolls—Fiction. | Adventure and adventurers—Fiction. | Magic—Fiction. | Secrets—Fiction. | Humorous stories.
Classification: LCC PZ7.C8344 Tr 2017 | DDC [Fic]—dc23

Printed in the United States of America
10 9 8 7 6 5 4 3 2 1
First Edition

Random House Children's Books supports the
First Amendment and celebrates the right to read.

For my faithful assistant,
Michael Ruffo

TROLLED

What You Should Know Before We Start

I think I should explain how what you're about to read came to be.

The main reason for my pages is that my sixth-grade teacher, Mr. Liebe, had this wacky idea that our class should spend the year writing biographies. He said it would be a great way to learn about the world, pick up some history, and better understand our families.

I thought it was pretty goofy, but holy heckenlooper, did I learn a lot about my family! Way more than I expected, in fact . . . and some of it pretty disturbing. I think I can say with certainty that we Takalas peg the needle on the weird-o-meter into the red zone in a way no one else in the class got near.

Anyway, because of Mr. Liebe's "Biography Project," I wrote a lot of what's here *while* it was happening. When things got really crazy, I kept writing—not for the project, just so I could keep track of the weirdness!

But what you'll find here is not entirely from me. I've mixed in a lot of stuff from other places . . . most especially from the diary of a certain N. Thump.

It took me a while to get some of the stranger stuff, which is the main reason it's taken me most of the year to finish this manuscript.

Now that it's done, I hope you'll enjoy it.

As for me, I'm just glad I survived!

No, that's not fair. Terrifying as this experience was at some points (and it was!), in the end I did more than survive.

I got something great out of it.

Actually, a lot of things, now that I think of it . . . most of them having to do with my family.

Oh, one more thing!

Given what's about to come, we should probably start with something from the world of the trolls.

Yeah, that's right.

Trolls.

Buckle your seat belt—we're about to take a wild and bumpy ride!

—Cody Takala

The Terrible Defiance of the Trolls!

1. Humans speak of rules and strictures.

    As trolls, we say "PBLPBLPBL" with all our tongues, no matter how many we have, flapping wildly above our chins!

2. The humans speak of laws and regulations.

    As trolls, we turn our backsides in order to unleash a mighty chorus of unified farts, as only seems appropriate.

3. The humans speak of honor and nobility.

    Considering that this comes from HUMANS, this causes us trolls to fall upon our backs and roll about, laughing until our stomachs hurt! Honor? Nobility? HUMANS?

    Our bellies cannot contain our mirth!

    We are trolls! And we think all humans should go sit upon the pinecone of their choice!

Permanent Resolution adopted at the Great Haudglazzim of 1541, recited (with sound effects) at every major troll gathering thereafter.

Tuesday, Sept. 6

My name is Ned Thump.

At least, that is what I am called these days, in this place.

It's close enough to my real name, I guess.

I am six feet eleven inches tall, weigh 345 pounds, and have a nose the size of a dill pickle.

My teeth are scraggly and of several different shapes.

Even so, I can pass for human.

At least, I can in New York City, where people are used to all sorts of strangeness. I may be one of the strangest the city has to offer, but being strange is so common here that people rarely give me a second look.

Well, maybe a second look, but almost never a third one.

Even so, on the rare nights when I am out and about in the upper world, I know I will hear rude comments about my looks.

I try not to let them bother me. After all, I'm not *supposed* to be good-looking by human standards. In fact, my size and face are two of the reasons I work as a night watchman, a job that lets me spend most of my time alone in the dark.

Which is fine with me.

So why start a diary now, in my one hundred and ninety-eighth year?

The answer is simple: I am lonely. And since I am stranded in the human world, the most likely candidate for someone to have a sensible conversation with is . . . me!

Actually, that would be true even if I were still in the Enchanted Realm, curse its rules and regulations. Generally speaking, my fellow trolls are not that interested in chitchat.

So, about the next two pages.

Because of all the trouble I had with my fifth-grade teacher, my mom was worried about what might happen in sixth grade. So in July she went charging into the school to get a look at my permanent record.

She told me she wanted to "head things off at the pass." (Whatever that means.)

Later I sorta, well . . . sorta found these and, um . . . sorta copied them.

Okay, let's not talk about that.

Mostly this seems like a good place to put them in, because this year I discovered there is actually a reason (a really weird one) that I'm good with animals and have a tendency to "sky."

—Cody

CODY TAKALA'S PERMANENT RECORD

Teacher Summary Comments, Grades 1–5

First Grade: Cody is a bright and eager student. It is a pleasure to have him in class, despite his occasional tendency to, shall we say, invent things. He is particularly good with our class rabbit, Bugs, who early on picked Cody as his favorite student. This created some jealousy among the other children, but I thought it spoke well of who Cody is. I believe animals are good judges of character.

—Ruth Hobek

Second Grade: Cody has two outstanding traits. The first is his impressive imagination, which does sometimes get him into trouble when he lets it run away with him. The second is his gift for working with animals. Our classroom gerbils seemed to adore him. Overall, he is a pleasant boy, and whoever gets him next year will be happy to have him as a student.

—Patty Parsons

Third Grade: Cody is obviously an intelligent child. However, his imagination is completely out of control and you cannot trust anything he tells you. I hope to goodness someone will clamp down on this before he gets himself into serious trouble! Also, he has been in a few fights this year when teased about his nickname, Rosie. (I have not been successful in finding out where the nickname came from.) Other than that, he is a pleasant enough boy.

—Irma Crisp

Fourth Grade: Cody has consistently delighted me with his creativity and storytelling skills. His writing has improved greatly from the beginning of the year, when he seemed reluctant, almost afraid, to give full rein to his imagination. Also, his care and tenderness with our classroom pets were extraordinary to witness. He is a gem, and any teacher will be lucky to have him as a student.

—Michael Denny

Fifth Grade: It would be hard to express the depths of my frustration with Cody. It seems he cannot go a single day without fabricating some wild story that has no root in reality. Though I had looked forward to having him in my room, his performance has gone steadily downhill throughout the year. He has been an enormous disappointment to me.

—Martin Savage

Cody here. After Mom got these, she found out something really cool about Mr. Liebe. He told her he doesn't look at the comments from previous teachers until he's had his class for at least two months. He said he prefers to form his own impression of the kids and that "prejudice" comes from "prejudging," which he tries to avoid.

Encyclopedia Enchantica

TROLLS

Trolls are, without a doubt, the Enchanted Realm's most difficult beings to describe. The reason is simple: whereas an elf is an elf is an elf, and unicorns are instantly recognizable, trolls come in a dizzying array of sizes and shapes, and even in numbers of heads.

And that doesn't begin to address the matter of whether such related groups as the hulder-folk and the tonttus fall under the broader term "troll."

This variety of forms is especially odd when you consider what a relatively small area (that part of northern Europe known as Scandinavia) the trolls occupy.

Some scholars believe that the first true trolls were descendants of the jotuns, those mighty giants who were in constant

Single-headed trolls are becoming more common.

Despite being on a single body, two heads may look completely different!

conflict with the Norse gods. This theory holds that at some point the creatures changed radically.

While there is no agreement on what would have prompted this, a handful of researchers suggest that the transformation was a reaction to the arrival of Christianity in the Northern Realms. They argue that the relatively swift change in the habits and beliefs of the humans provoked a crisis in trolldom. A handful even maintain that this change is ongoing.

That idea is, of course, wildly controversial.

Yet there is no denying the strange connection between humans and trolls. Whatever the reason for the enormous variety in which trolls appear, the fact of that variety is enough to busy even the hardest-working scholar for a lifetime.

Gertrud Albusmiss
Elfen Princess and Troll Specialist
University Enchantica
Paris Branch

- -

Sept. 7

Annual Employee Evaluation:

Ned Thump

As I have stated every year since I first took over this office, Ned Thump is an exceptional employee. He is honest, loyal, and completely reliable. In my years here he has never missed a night of work. He always arrives on time and never leaves early.

More significantly, Ned's remarkable size (he's HUGE!), combined with his astonishing speed and his uncanny ability to move in the dark, makes him a superb night watchman. Few troublemakers are brave enough to challenge him, and the ones who do are amazed when this enormous man catches them so quickly.

As I am required to suggest areas for improvement, I will note that some of Ned's fellow workers are bothered by the way he sticks to himself and does not interact with them. I have asked Ned to try being more of a team player, but I understand that he is a loner by nature and finds this difficult.

I have also found that Ned can be resistant to change. He very much likes things—such as the order of his rounds—to stay as they are. However, he accepts orders without complaint, even when it is obvious that he is not happy about them.

In summary: Though Ned's size and unusual appearance can be disconcerting, it should be obvious that they are also highly useful for this particular job. I wish I had a dozen more like him!

Peter Takala
Supervisor, Night Division
Security Department

PERFORMANCE CHART:
Ned Thump

	Excellent	Good	Needs Improvement	Poor
Promptness	X			
Reliability	X			
Team Player			X	
Enthusiasm	X			
Attitude		X		
Communication Skills		X		
Flexibility			X	
Attendance Record	X!!			

Thursday, Sept. 8

I like big words, words such as "felicific," "pusillanimous," and "deviated septum." (All right, that last is two words. But you have to admit they tumble sweetly off the tongue.)

This love of multisyllables is one more thing that made me an outcast among my fellow trolls, whose idea of witty mockery might be a conversation like this:

Troll 1: "You smell too nice. Stupid troll!"
Troll 2: "You talk too pretty. Stupid troll!"
Troll 1: "Stinky face!"
Troll 2: "Funny butt!"
Troll 1: "Nose drooler!"
Troll 2: "Tiny farter!!!"

"Tiny farter" is, of course, the worst thing you can call a troll.

It would all be downhill after that.

So though I accept that I am terrible at being a troll, I am not entirely unhappy at being stranded here in the human world.

At least the insults are more interesting.

Sept. 9

Dear Parents and Guardians,

I wanted to let you know early on about one of the most important aspects of this year's curriculum. I have been granted permission by the school board to proceed with a new program called "The Biography Project."

This exciting approach unites some of the most important aspects of learning—reading, writing, history, and research—in a connected series of ongoing tasks.

The basic idea is that the best way to learn about the world is to learn about people. With that in mind, the students will write numerous biographies throughout the year. Some will be of historical figures. Others will be of current leaders or celebrities. Still others will be of people within the student's own circle—family members, friends, perhaps work acquaintances suggested by either Mom or Dad.

Most important, the project will begin and end with the students writing their autobiographies.

Awareness begins from within and expands outward from there. It is my hope and expectation that the second autobiography will display considerable growth, both personal and academic, on the part of your children.

Please be assured that this approach is fully compliant with state standards.

Normal curriculum for math and science will prevail . . . though I will try to integrate those areas as much as possible with our biography work.

To be clear: the biography project will involve more writing than usual. It will also require the students to interact more fully with the world outside of school. I hope you will support your student in these endeavors.

Adventure and discovery await us!

If you have any questions, please do not hesitate to contact me. I am almost always available for conferences and consults in the hour after the school day ends.

Yours in education,

Herb Liebe

Saturday, Sept. 10

Years ago I had to have a photograph taken in order to get my security badge for work.

Unlike some of my relatives, I can handle light well enough, at least for a short time. But the blinding flash when the picture was snapped nearly made me pass out!

I sincerely hope I never have to do that again.

I am pasting a copy of the photo in here, as a reminder of a particularly awful day.

Ned Thump
Night Security

TROLLS AND LIGHT

From *The Complete Guide
to Trolls and Their Ways*

It is widely believed in the human world that sunlight is fatal to trolls. As with many things humans believe, this idea contains a kernel of truth wrapped in a fantasia of nuttery.

It *is* true that sunlight could be lethal for earlier generations of trolls. Hundreds of years ago, a troll foolish enough to be out and about after the sun rose *might* be turned into stone (which is to say, returned to its essence). The important thing to note is that this was not true of *all* trolls.

Professor Elmgarden (dwarf), in a decades-long study, proved a definite connection between lack of intelligence and the likelihood of being petrified by sunlight. The reason for this is not clear, but the result was that the trolls most likely to turn to stone were also the ones most likely to be caught outside at daybreak. And the trolls *least* likely to turn to stone were the ones who *most* avoided sunlight to begin with.

Naturally, the population of trolls subject to petrification dwindled. After a number of centuries they nearly disappeared altogether.

Even so, it took a long period of careful (and sometimes fatal) exploration for the remaining trolls to realize that sunlight was no longer deadly for most of them.

Which is not to say that it is pleasant. Bright light of any kind is uncomfortable for all trolls. Extended exposure can result in a painful "lightburn"—something that makes a human sunburn seem pale by comparison!

To summarize: while trolls are generally happier and more comfortable in the darkness, they *can* be out in the world if necessary . . . though doing so may come at a painful cost.

Markus Karlsen, Dwarf
Professor of Interspecies Studies
University Enchantica

Monday, Sept. 12

One of the best things about my job is that it gives me a legitimate reason to terrorize humans! Only bad humans, of course . . . but there are more than enough of them to satisfy my taste for this.

Truly, few things are as delightful as spotting a crook or an intruder somewhere in Grand Central Terminal and then using my troll-stealth to sneak up behind him. I love the way they scream in surprise! Even better is the way mere fright changes to bone-freezing terror when they turn and see my face!

I do not think I will ever get tired of this.

It almost makes up for having had to leave home.

Writing Prompt

"MY MOST EMBARRASSING MOMENT"

What I want you to think about today is the most embarrassing thing that ever happened to you . . . and how it has affected you. Are you changed because of it? Are there things you no longer try? Are there things you do differently?

This is an unusual assignment because I do NOT want you to turn it in! The reason is simple—I don't want you to be shy about writing this, which you probably would be if you thought I was going to see it. So you are on your honor on this one. I will never know whether you do it or not.

But I hope you will. I think you may discover things that will be very useful as you work on your autobiography . . . which is, I remind you, due next Wednesday!

—Mr. L

F. L. Atul

UNITED PHYSICIANS (U.P.)
PHYSICIANS PLAZA (P.P.)
Water Street
New York, NY 10004

September 15

Dear Mr. and Mrs. Takala:

After my appointment with Cody last week, I did quite a bit of research on his unusual condition. Unfortunately, I could find nothing in the medical literature that touches on this.

I do understand that Cody finds the condition embarrassing. However, as he is otherwise extremely healthy, I do not think you should worry about it.

Sincerely,

F. L. Atul

Pediatrician

Thursday, Sept. 15

Another good thing about my job is that I actually like my boss, Mr. Peter Takala.

It seems an amazing piece of luck that I am able to work for someone who also has family roots in Finland. Though, of course, Mr. T (as all of us night watchmen call him) comes from the human world in Finland, not the Enchanted Realm.

The downside of having Mr. T as my boss is that he has a son who makes me nervous. The boy—his name is Cody—is nice enough. But he seems to be extremely curious about me.

The last thing I need is some boy snooping around trying to discover my true story!

My Most Embarrassing Moment

Boy, Mr. Liebe really came up with a tough one this time. Thank goodness we don't have to hand it in!

Mr. L is smart that way. He knows if he asked us to give him a paper called "My Most Embarrassing Moment," hardly anyone would write something honest. It would be too . . . well, *embarrassing!*

So he wants us to write this just for ourselves. I'm sure he knows some of us won't bother. But I love that he leaves it up to us.

As for me, I didn't have to think very long to know what I had to write about. And it's not my farts. They're embarrassing, but also kind of funny.

This is way more serious, and something I definitely wouldn't hand in.

Good grief. This is even harder to put down than I thought it would be. I wonder if that's because writing it down makes it more real somehow.

Okay, it was fourth grade. Springtime.

I was planning to walk home with Bud Parker, who is kind of cool in some ways, but also a total geekling. (Sometimes the two things go together.) We had gone only a block past the school when we were surrounded by a pack of sixth graders out for blood.

Not mine. Bud's.

Why they were after him I have no idea. I don't know if they did, either. One weird thing was that I knew some of the kids in the group, and they were basically good kids. At least, that was what I thought. But somehow the pack thing had changed that.

"Hey, nerdbutt," said Derek Curtis. "Going off to a nerdfest?"

Which he seemed to think was brilliant.

I don't want to go into all of this. The only thing I have to write down is my own complete embarrassment, which I still feel two years later.

Because I did nothing.

I said nothing.

I let those creeps pick on, tease, and humiliate Bud.

And I did . . . nothing.

When I think about it, it makes me sick. Who was I on that day? Whoever it was, I don't want to be that kid, that Cody, ever again, on any day.

It's not who I am!

No, that's not really true. It is who I was.

But I don't want to be that kid again.

Ever.

That's not how a hero acts.

Thanks a lot, Mr. Liebe. Now I'm kind of sick to my stomach.

Even so, I guess I needed to think about that day, which I've mostly been trying not to. It's important that I never forget it.

God, I'm glad I don't have to hand this in.

Saturday, Sept. 17

Saturday nights are hard.

That is because for the humans, Saturday is "Date Night" . . . a cause for fun and frolic.

The thought that I could ever have a date is sadly hilarious, for more than one reason. So, accepting that I will be alone, it is a good night to write.

What I want to write about tonight is my home.

To start with, I live underground.

This is good, as it feels more natural than would living "up above."

On the other hand, most of the tunnels down here are not natural. They are part of the train and subway system, so definitely man-made. (Well, man-made and troll-made. I personally helped excavate many of them!)

I am not the only one who dwells beneath the city. Many humans live down here, too. They have a number of loose communities.

These "undergrounders" accept me more easily than do the humans who walk the streets above us. I guess we outcasts recognize each other.

That doesn't mean we interact a lot. Even underground, I am, as would be expected, on the outer edge of things.

Which is the way it needs to be.

Though most of the tunnel people are friendly enough, the rule seems to be that you don't ask questions about why anyone is here. Which is fine with me! Generally, we leave each other alone. The exception is when someone finds a nice batch of discarded restaurant food that can be shared around.

I find I have developed a fondness for pasta.

Mostly, however, I eat rats. They are plentiful, easy to catch, and quite tasty if properly prepared.

The undergrounders call them track rabbits.

I could buy my own food, of course, since I have a job. But why pay for food when rats are so available? They are good raw, but I have also developed many tasty recipes to give myself some variety in my diet. My favorite is a rat-and-vegetable stew I call ratatouille. (I got the name from some human dish, but I don't think that one actually uses rats, which seems kind of silly.)

I do have a special friend among the humans, a little girl named Martha. She is seven years old and lives down here with her mother.

I do not know why the two of them have chosen to live underground.

As I said, we don't ask questions.

Sometimes I bring fresh food for Martha and her mother. This makes the mother (I forget her name) happy. Other times I buy Martha small gifts—toys and coloring books, mostly.

This seems to me a good way to spend some of the money I make.

Martha thinks "Pull My Finger" is the funniest game ever invented. This is something I agree with.

Of course, given the power of my trollish farts, playing "Pull My Finger" raises the game to a whole new level.

Martha's mother was afraid of me at first. But after I protected her and her daughter a couple of times when trouble was brewing, she relaxed and began to trust me.

It is nice to have someone to take care of.

Good grief. What an untrollish thought!

Sometimes I fear I am getting infected with human feelings.

Perhaps the time is coming when I should go home.

Hah! What a ridiculous idea.

Even so, I can't help but wonder what would happen if I tried. . . .

Sunday, Sept. 18

I hate shoes!

I am thinking about this because tomorrow I have to go back to work.

That mostly makes me happy, as I like my job. But there is one bad thing about this. It means that tomorrow I have to put my shoes back on.

And I hate shoes! Not only are they uncomfortable, they hide my wonderful foot smell!

What makes it worse is that I don't even need the dratted things. My feet are so tough I can walk across broken glass without pain or injury. But I am forced to wear the cramping, pinching, nasty, sweat-inducing things for my job. Even if they weren't required by my boss, I would need them to hide the talons that grow from the ends of my broad and hairy toes.

Humans are so sensitive! If they would walk around in bare feet all the time, they would toughen up soon enough and not have to worry about wasting money on these toe-squashing leather monstrosities!

Speaking of money, my shoes are real wallet-drainers. That's because my feet are so big I have to have my shoes custom made. (Few humans, even ones of my height, have feet as big as mine!)

The first thing I do each morning when I get back to my cave is tear off the wretched leather foot prisons and let my poor aching toes breathe and stretch!

Humans are strange, and if I had had any doubt on that matter, the issue of shoes has settled it.

9/18

Tonight was very weird.

And upsetting.

It started out with me trying to do something I thought was really good. Though I wouldn't tell this to Mr. Liebe, his Biography Project has got me thinking about my own family and how much I don't know about them.

For example: What is Great-Granny Aino's story? Why did she and Great-Grampa Harald (who I never met because he died before I was born) move to America to begin with? And most important, what happened between Dad and Grampa Raimo? Why aren't we in contact with him?

If I'm going to understand my family, these are things I should know. So tonight after supper I went over to talk to Granny Aino. (That's what I call her. We've agreed to skip the "great" part. She says it depresses her.)

I thought it was going to be fun, but what actually happened was pretty awful.

Things started out well enough. Norman the Doorman greeted me with his usual "Hey, Codester, how's your roadster?" Which is basically ridiculous, since (a) I'm too young to drive, (b) even if I wasn't, I probably wouldn't drive in NYC, and (c) who calls a car a roadster anymore, anyway?

It should be annoying. But Norman is so cheerful that I don't mind his totally goofy way of greeting me.

Plus, I know he takes good care of Granny Aino, which counts for a lot.

He used the house phone to tell her I was on my way up, so she was waiting at her door when I got to the penthouse.

"Oh, look!" she cried happily. "My little tonttu has come to visit!"

A tonttu is some sort of dwarfy creature from Finland.

If anyone else tried to call me this, I'd be annoyed. But since it's Granny Aino, it's all right. And it's a heck of a lot better than Rosie, my stupid nickname at school.

"Come on in and have a seat," she said.

I went straight to my favorite chair, which is so soft that when you sit down it's like getting hugged.

As soon as I had settled in, Askeladden jumped into my lap and started to purr.

His full name is actually Askeladden III, since he's the third cat of this sort that Granny Aino has had. He's a big guy, with a ridiculously thick silver and gray coat. His name comes from some Norwegian folktales—which is a bit odd, since we're Finnish, not Norwegian. But Granny says magic is magic, cats are cats, and she'll call her cat whatever she darn well pleases.

Once Askeladden was in place, Granny offered me some cookies. She is, I swear, the world's greatest cookie-maker! Her specialty is Finnish Spoon Cookies with Cloudberry Jam. OMG, they are sooooo good.

(My friends say cloudberry jam is something I made up and I'm just skying when I tell them about it. But it's a real thing in Finland.)

Next Gran asked her usual questions about how I was doing, did I have a girlfriend yet (Blurtch! As if!), what were my grades like, and so on.

Once we got past all that, I started to tell her about the Biography Project. As I got deeper into it, her hands started to tremble so badly that she sloshed tea out of her cup.

I probably should have shut up right then.

Unfortunately, shutting up has never been my strong point. So I said, "Anyway, all that got me thinking, and I realized I know hardly anything about your life before you came to America. So I wanted to ask you about it. And about what happened with Grampa Raimo."

She dropped her cup. But instead of springing to her feet to deal with the spill, she closed her eyes and said softly, "I'd rather not have this conversation, Cody."

Her voice was sad, but very firm.

"Did I do something wrong?" I asked.

She bent to pick up the fallen teacup, which let her

avoid my eyes. "No, you've done nothing wrong, dear. Even so, you'd better go now. I need to clean up this mess."

"I'll help you," I said.

"No!" she said, her voice sharper now. "I'll take care of it. Please, Cody, you need to go now."

I almost started to cry. Clearly I *had* done something wrong. But what?

Whatever it was, I didn't want to make things any worse. So I held in my tears and left.

But, seriously, what the holy heckenlooper was THAT about???

And why do I feel so terrible when I can't even figure out what I did to upset her?

Tuesday, Sept. 20

I have decided to write some things about my past. That's because I have been looking at *A Troddler's Guide to Life,* the book I brought with me when I left Troll Mountain to come to America. It was a book that I loved, and it brings back many memories.

I lived in terror of my father. Fortunately, I did not have to see him that much, since he was always busy being king. My mother terrified me as well. As I was her only child, she expected much of me.

But children will be children, whether trolls or humans, and despite the fear I felt at home (my mother's lullabies were terrifying), I played and laughed with my troddler friends. We happily annoyed our elders by running races through the mountain passages. And there is probably no better place in the world for hide-and-seek than the inside of Troll Mountain. Oh, the nooks! Oh, the crannies!

Also, there were the animals. Troll Mountain is filled with cats, and they were very good to talk to. (To be honest, they were more intelligent than many of the trolls . . . especially the three-headers, who have to share one brain divided into thirds.)

I do miss the kitties.

The other animals we had in abundance were ravens,

which were trained from shortly after hatching to be messengers between the troll kingdoms. Like cats, the ravens were able to talk to us. I had several good friends among them. They also liked big words, which was a deliciousness we shared.

When I was young I also had many friends among the tonttus. Though most tonttus live in the forests, we did have a tribe inside Troll Mountain. And a good thing, since the tonttus actually did much of the important work, being generally far more sensible than trolls.

When we were young our size difference was not so great. But as we grew older the tonttus topped out at about three feet, whereas we trolls kept growing, and growing, and . . . well, let's just say that at nearly seven feet, I am only medium height.

This size difference became more of an issue the larger it grew. I hated that it seemed to make the trolls feel they could order the tonttus around, in ways that were sometimes cruel. I tried to stand up for the little people, but it was not always easy.

I had one special friend among them, a particularly clever tonttu named Aspen. We got into a great deal of mischief together, especially when we would sneak out of the mountain to visit the human world. Sadly, that eventually led to our being separated, since we got caught at it one time too many. My father was furious and decreed that I was no longer allowed to play with Aspen. It was only my pleading that saved my friend from a beating.

Well, all that was long ago. But I still think of it often. Some things, I think, never go away.

Wednesday, Sept. 21

THIS IS ME
By Cody Takala

My name is Cody Takala. I am eleven years old and have just started the sixth grade.

My father's family comes from Finland, and we are very proud of our Finnish heritage. We love America, but sometimes we think Finland is more sensible in the way it handles things. (I am sort of quoting my great-grandmother, Aino Takala, on this. I will write more about her later.)

Sometimes people hear my last name and think I must be part Japanese. That is because there is a surprising similarity between the Japanese and Finnish languages. However, it is mostly in sound, not word meaning or how it is written.

No one knows why this is.

My father is in charge of Night Security for Grand Central Terminal, which is, in my opinion, the greatest building in the history of the world. (Most people call it Grand Central Station, but that is not the real name.

It's properly called a terminal because so many trains end—terminate—there.)

My mother is a pianist/singer and performs at hotels and clubs in New York City. Her name is Mala, which is Indian (as in India-Indian).

Mala is actually her middle name. Her first name is Dorothy. My Aunt Ellen, who is Mom's sister, likes to bust on her about this. She says Mom only married Dad because she thought Mala Takala would be a great name for a performer.

Mom says if that was all she wanted she could have changed her name without going through the trouble of getting married.

Mom can be pretty snarky.

Since Mom and Dad both work at night, I often go to Dad's office at Grand Central with him. This is because Mom considers her workplaces "inappropriate" for me (meaning she doesn't want me hanging around in bars). Happily, I am welcome at Dad's place as long as I don't interfere with his work. I have a cot in his office where I can sleep, and a small desk of my own so I can do homework. I know a lot of the security guards by name. It's pretty cool.

But don't think I always have to go to work with Dad. My grandfather on my mother's side lives with us, so I can stay home with him if I want. Grampa used to work in a circus (I'm not skying about this!) and he traveled all over the world performing. So Mom being in show business comes naturally.

To be honest, I am happier about Grampa living with us than Mom is. I know she loves him. But she also thinks he is exasperating.

(Mr. Liebe—you told us we should be completely honest in these essays, so I am counting on you NOT showing this to my mother!!)

Another thing I am lucky about is that my *great*-grandmother on Dad's side lives only a few blocks away. I totally love her, even if she is slightly strange. Most of my friends only have grandparents. Only a few have a great-grandparent, and I bet not one of them is as cool as Granny Aino. And that's not just because she's rich, though she is. You should see her apartment! She has the most ginormous wall-screen TV I have ever seen. Sometimes I get to stay over and watch movies on it, which is awesome.

I will tell one odd thing about her. We have pictures from when she was young, and she looked like a movie star. Heck, she looked BETTER than most movie stars!

Not anymore.

(Okay, Mr. Liebe, I'm asking you again to be true to your word and keep this private! If you don't, I'm dead.)

The truth is, somewhere along the way my great-grandmother got pretty homely. It's weird to compare how she looks now with how she looked way back when.

I have scanned in a couple of pictures so that you can see the difference.

It doesn't really matter, of course. After all, great-grammas aren't supposed to be beauty queens!

It also doesn't matter because Granny Aino is the best and sweetest person in the world!

Seriously.

Even so, I'm always puzzled by what happened to her.

One more thing about Granny Aino: she is responsible for my special talent. I can speak Finnish! That's because from the time I was born she spoke to me only in that language. It's not something I get to practice a lot, but I am glad I can do it. I hope to go to Finland someday. That would be cool. (And not just because of the climate, ha ha.)

Okay, on to my life today. Mom says I am a New Yorker born and bred. I suppose it's true, because I have lived here all my life. I know some people think the city is scary, but I can't understand that. If you don't go where you shouldn't, when you shouldn't, New York is very safe.

Mom takes me to the theater a lot. Sometimes we see Broadway shows, which I love! Other times we go to little theaters down in Greenwich Village. Those shows are a "mixed bag." Some are truly amazing. Others leave me going "HUH?"

Mom says the "Huh?" shows are good for me.

Dad says they will be my downfall.

My parents do not always agree. But they really do love each other, which makes me happy.

More about me: I like to tell stories, sometimes more than I should. I call this skying. I'm really good at it, but sometimes it gets me in trouble. My last year's teacher, *who I will not name because he was so mean to me,* used to get really mad about it. Sometimes he would yell at me so bad it made me cry. I always felt stupid when that happened.

I am pretty good at sports, but not totally crazy about them.

My favorite comic book is Spider-Man, and my

favorite movie is *Guardians of the Galaxy*. (I love Groot!!)

The thing I hate most is bullies.

When I grow up I would like to be a hero who saves someone. Or maybe a veterinarian. That would be cool, too.

I am Cody Takala, and that is all I have to say about myself for now. And you'd better keep it secret or I will never trust you again!

Cody—

This was fascinating. I think you have a very good life, and I am glad that you appreciate it. And don't worry, this essay was just to help me get to know you. I promise I will not spill your secrets!

—Mr. L

Thursday, Sept. 22

I want to talk more about my home.

I live underneath—*way* underneath—the most beautiful building in the world.

At least, it's the most beautiful building I've ever seen. It's called Grand Central Terminal and it is a wonder and a glory. Its central area is like a vast, man-made cavern . . . only aboveground!

Painted across its arched ceiling, 125 feet above the station floor, is a mural of the constellations. Something few people know is that the constellations are reversed. Goodness, was there some unhappiness when that was first noticed! Made me glad I had been digging tunnels rather than painting skies!

Something else about that ceiling. Over the years it had become increasingly dark as the paint was covered with grime. Everyone thought it was soot from the trains . . . until they cleaned it several years ago and discovered that what actually turned the ceiling dark was the smoke from hundreds of millions of cigarettes! True story!

I could go on and on—there is so much that is wonderful about this building. But fantastic as it is, it's what lies *underneath* Grand Central that really matters to me. Hardly anyone knows about this. Only someone like me, who is comfortable underground and in the dark, can really understand it.

Here is how I became part of the world of Grand Central.

I came to America in the mid-1800s (as humans reckon time). There were masses of us coming from Finland then, so many that it was easy for me to pass as human in the throngs.

Even though I was passing, I was always noticed, since I was invariably the biggest, ugliest person in any group. (I wasn't really a "person," of course, but I needed to pretend I was. I don't think they were letting trolls through Immigration.)

I tried not to let the way people looked at me hurt, but it was hard . . . especially given the reason I had to leave the Enchanted Realm to begin with.

Pah! I do not want to talk about *that* now . . . or probably ever. I will say only that when I departed from Troll Mountain I felt as if my heart had been sliced in two. But I had to go, because I was no longer safe there. So, with my mother's reluctant help, I joined the great migration. It was the best way to save me from my father's wrath, and one of the few good things she ever did for me.

I was lucky in my timing. . . . I arrived in America as the first Grand Central (there have actually been two of them!) was being built. With all the underground work needed, it was a perfect place for a troll to get a job. Being large and remarkably strong (by human standards), I easily found work with the excavation crews.

Oh, the digging! Oh, the tunneling! You would have thought men had become trolls, the way they burrowed, burrowed, burrowed through some of the hardest rock I had ever seen.

It was demanding work, but I loved it.

Now, here is the important part: as I worked, I watched and waited. Eventually, as I had hoped, I found a way through one of the stone walls to a hidden set of caves.

These I claimed as my home.

In the years since then, using my trollish skills, I have made my private space quite comfortable . . . so comfortable that a number of undergrounders have tried to steal it.

That does not happen much anymore. Word has gotten around about how scary I can be. That's partly because the last time someone tried to steal my place, it did not end well for him.

The memory of his terrified squeals still makes me happy.

I love my home.

I would love it more if I had someone to share it with, but that seems an impossible dream. Certainly it could never be with the one I loved so much that I lost all.

I try not to think about that. My home is of stone, and my heart must be as well or it would surely break in two.

Or perhaps shatter into a million pieces.

Pah! Why do I write such simpering things? I am a troll. My heart is not soft and stupid! It is a thing of stone!

Well, mostly of stone.

It does have a soft spot. Which was the source of my shame, and why I had to flee Troll Mountain.

About Troll Mountain

From *A Troddler's Guide to Life*

Troll Mountain exists in both the human world and the Enchanted Realm.

In the human world it is mountain through and through, with a small number of caves and tunnels.

However, in the Enchanted Realm the mountain houses a vast and thriving world of caves, caverns, hidey-holes, and passages. For those of us who live here, Troll Mountain's exterior is much like an eggshell for a gigantic egg . . . a thin, protective coat that shields and protects all the life packed inside.

Many passages lead out of the mountain to the human world. A troll can pass through them to tromp about among people whenever he or she wants . . . though despite the agitation by younger trolls for a world-merger, we do that tromping about less often these days.

Of course, those passages lead into the mountain as well, but only for trolls! Unless a human has a special guide, or a key to enter, when he or she enters one, all that will be seen is a short tunnel ending at a solid wall. Yet a troll who passes through the very same opening will be once more in the Enchanted Realm, and can roam the mountain at will.

(Author unknown)

Human view

Troll view

JEAN SIBELIUS SCHOOL FOR THE ARTS
W. 83RD ST., NEW YORK, NY
"Art is Life. Life is Art!"

Friday, Sept. 23

Dear Mr. and Mrs. Takala,

I am truly enjoying having Cody in my class. He is cheerful, quite bright, and very creative. His autobiography was lively and witty.

Unfortunately, his creativity tends to get the better of him on occasion, which is why I am writing to you now.

To be blunt, Cody has a tendency to . . . well, to tell stories.

Let me be clear. He does not do this with bad intent. And often the tales are quite amusing, if not entirely believable. When I—or one of his classmates—call him on his yarns, he will smile and say, "Heck, I'm just skying."

I hesitate to call this lying. In most cases Cody is quite truthful. For example: if something goes wrong and I ask if he was involved, I can count on a straight answer. He does not tell tales to get out of trouble. He just does it because . . . well, it's as if he can't help himself.

His classmates are mostly amused by this . . . mostly, but not always. Some are getting frustrated by his tendency to "sky." Last week we had a minor incident when I read the class a story from a collection of tales gathered by Raimo Takala, a Finnish folklorist.

When I was done reading, Cody tried to tell everyone that Raimo is his grandfather, that he is the world's most important authority on Finnish folklore, and that he has published over twenty books and collected dozens of previously unknown folktales.

Since Cody talked a great deal about his family in his autobiography but did not even mention this famous grandfather, it seems likely he was skying again.

I truly do appreciate Cody's creativity. However, I felt I should alert you to the possibility that he may suffer some social backlash from his proclivity for spinning a yarn.

You might want to have a word with him.

Sincerely,

Herb Liebe

Saturday, Sept. 24

I have found that writing in this diary does seem to help with my loneliness. Which is odd, since at the same time it is making me aware of how lonely I really am.

I wish I could go home.

NO! Stop. That is foolish.

Why would I want to go back to that cruelty?

Because it *is* home? Or, more accurately, *used* to be home?

What is it that makes me long for Troll Mountain . . . and even for Mother and Father, despite how badly they treated me?

That's a useless question, given that going home could never happen. Mother would never allow it. And Father would . . . well, I don't even want to think about that!

I wonder if they are even still alive.

Probably. We trolls live a long time.

On the other hand, I am fairly certain—no, completely certain—that my friend is gone.

So what reason would I have to return?

Text messages between Alexandra Carhart and Cody Takala

Alex
Hey, Rosie, how you doin'?

Cody
Don't call me that!

Alex
Sorry, Cuz. Can't help myself. It's so funny!

Cody
Funny for everyone but me. You got a reason for this text, or you just want to annoy me?

Alex
Annoying you is a happy side effect. Mostly I wanted to nudge about Destiny's b-day party. You guys comin'?

Cody
I hope so! Depends on if Mom has a gig the night before.

Alex
Family first!

Cody
Mom mostly feels that way. But sometimes show biz comes first.

Alex
Aunt Mala needs to get her priorities straight!

Cody

I'll bust her on that and see what I can do.

Alex

You've got 3 weeks. Make it happen!

Cody

I'll TRY!

Alex

Good. That makes you my favorite cousin.

Cody

I'm your only cousin.

Alex

Yeah, but even if I had other cousins they wouldn't be able to do that hilarious fart thing.

Cody

You only think it's hilarious because you don't have to live with it.

Alex

You wouldn't believe some of the things I live with these days.

Cody

Like what?

Alex

Skip it. Focus on the party. Be here or be branded a doot!

Cody

Anything but that!!

Alex

Beware the fate of the doot!

Cody

I'll talk to Mom!!

Alex

Yer the best, Codes. Love ya.

Cody

Eeeeuuuuuuwwwww!

Alex

Hah! Got you!

Sunday, Sept. 25

I realize my entries have been sounding rather bleak lately, so I should add that I do have some pleasures in my life.

For example, there is farting.

Truly, few things are more satisfying than surprising someone with a fart. In our underground world, I have developed a reputation for my huge and deadly ones.

"Ned!" the others will cry when we have a newcomer to the community. "Ned, come here and cut the cheese for this guy!"

Everyone loves to count how many echoes I can get.

To be honest, my farts would be no more than average in the kingdoms of the trolls. But here among the humans they are what would be called world-class.

If there were an Olympic category for farting, I could blow away the competition!

Hmmmm. I think I will go up above tonight and have some "fartertainment."

The results when I let a few go at the movies can be hilarious!

Sept. 26

Dear Mr. Liebe—

I appreciated your note and kind words about Cody. Let me assure you, his dad and I are well aware of his tendency to "sky." How could we not be, after all the problems we had over it with his teacher last year?

And we do understand that this gives him a problem with credibility.

However, in this case I must protest on Cody's behalf. The fact is, Raimo Takala is indeed Cody's grandfather, and truly is one of the world's foremost scholars of Finnish folklore. His collection *Secret Stories of Scandinavia* has been translated into thirty-five languages.

I suspect the reason Cody did not mention this in his autobiography is that Raimo moved to Finland more than twenty-five years ago and has not stayed in close touch with the family. The situation has been hurtful to Cody's dad, and we do not talk about Raimo much, even though we have most of his books on our shelves.

I want to assure you that Cody loves being in your class and is excited about the Biography Project. So I hope you can quickly put an end to any friction with the class on the matter of his grandfather.

Sincerely,

Mala Takala

Tuesday, Sept. 27

I fear I was lying to myself when I said I don't let comments about my looks bother me.

They do.

Why should this be? I am a troll. I am supposed to be ugly! I am even supposed to be proud of my ugliness!

But I am not living among trolls, and that changes things.

Is being surrounded by all these humans rubbing off on me?

Sometimes I worry that I am developing human emotions.

What a horrifying thought!

Next thing you know, I'll be writing poetry!

Rules for Troll Poetry

1) Poems must rhyme.
2) It is acceptable to invent words to create a rhyme.
3) The proper rhythm is:
   BOMP diddy BOMP diddy BOMP diddy BOMP.
4) The rhyme scheme can be AB AB AB (cat/dog, rat/fog, mat/clog) or AA BB CC (cat/rat, dog/fog, nose/blows).
5) Every poem must contain at least one fart!

Sample of an AA BB CC poem:

What *did you* **do** *when you* **went** *to the* **school?**
Chased *all the* **chil**-*dren till* **I** *made them* **drool.**
Picked *up the* **big**-*gest and* **gave** *him a* **squeeze.**
Fart *came so* **hard** *that it* **caused** *a big* **breeze!**
What *did you* **do** *when you* **got** *yourself* **home?**
Put *a hat* **on** *my cat,* **then** *wrote this* **pome!**

From *A Troll's Guide to Verse and Worse*
By Albemarl Fractus
Fourteenth Edition

Oh, Cruel World!

Why *did I* come *to this* strange *foreign* land?
I *had no* choice, *I was* sent *by de-*mand!
Made *a mis-*take *and was* told *I must* pay;
Pun-*ishment* lasts *up through* this *very* day!
Sent *to the* world *where the* hu-*mans must* live,
Two *hundred* years *later* should *I for-*give?
No, *I will* not! *I've a* stone *for a* heart!
I *will for-*give *when a* moun-*tain can* fart!

By Ned Thump
(My First Poem!)

9/28

Today Mr. Liebe came up with our next biography assignment. We're supposed to choose the most unusual person we know, even if we don't know him or her well, then gather enough information to write their life story.

My first thought was to write about my grandfather. After all, he used to work in a circus, which is fairly unusual. And he can still put one foot behind his head—definitely unusual for a guy who's almost seventy! Also, he can juggle coconuts. (He has to do it outside, though, on account of Mom got upset about the dents in the ceiling.)

On the other hand, using him seems a little like cheating, since he lives right here.

Then I thought about Ned Thump, one of Dad's night watchmen at Grand Central.

Ned is the weirdest-*looking* person I've ever met. To begin with, he's so big they have to have his uniforms custom made. Dad told me he didn't mind the cost because Ned's size alone is enough to scare off bad guys. "And that would be before they get a look at his face!" he added—which was not very nice, but true. Once you get past the size of Ned's schnoz, you start to notice the warts, the gigantic bushy eyebrows, and the super-wide mouth with the scraggly teeth.

It's hard not to stare. I mean, I try not to, because I know it's rude. But really, you've never seen anyone like him!

Another thing: Ned is real quiet—which in New York City is pretty unusual all on its own!

Also, there is something weirdly familiar about his name. That doesn't make much sense, but it keeps nagging at the back of my mind.

Next time I go to work with Dad, I'll see if I can find Ned and interview him. Could be interesting!

Thursday, Sept. 29

I don't know if it is good to use this diary to get out my resentments, or if doing so will only make them fester more, but I can't help myself tonight.

What got me started on this was watching Martha play with one of the dolls I brought her. It's called a Barbie, and it is absurdly pretty.

This got me to thinking about the hulder-maids, who are part of the troll realm. And that thinking fills my heart with rage, because instead of being hideous, like me, huldra are absurdly pretty.

I would say that humans are insanely obsessed with looks and appearance. But the truth is, I am, too.

Given my face, at least *I* have a reason!

9/30

This evening Dad let me go to his office with him. Once he was involved in his work, I took off to wander the terminal, hoping to spot Ned.

It wouldn't be that hard to find him in most places . . . he is definitely a guy who stands out. But that doesn't take into account how huge GCT is. There are dozens of platforms for the trains, and over a hundred shops and restaurants.

Fortunately, I knew some of the places Ned was most likely to be stationed. After about an hour, I spotted him in one of the lower tunnels.

He waved when he saw me, which seemed like a good sign. But he was clearly surprised when I walked toward him.

"Can I help you, Cody?" he asked.

His voice was like a rumble of thunder.

"I hope so!" I said, trying to sound cheerful. "I'm supposed to do a report on an interesting person for school. I think *you're* interesting, so I would like to interview you."

Ned's eyes bulged out in a way I would not have thought humanly possible, and he said, "Please don't ask me that!"

Then he turned and hurried away.

It made me think of the way that Granny Aino had reacted when I wanted to ask about *her* history.

Is everyone I know hiding something?

Naturally, Ned's reaction made me even more curious about him (probably the opposite of what he wanted). However, it was also a little frightening. Though I wouldn't have thought *anything* could scare Ned Thump, he had looked terrified.

Is he hiding some deep, dark secret? Like, is he some kind of fugitive criminal?

Or is he just shy because he's so ugly?

Wow. I just realized how rough middle school must have been for him.

Poor guy.

Probably the smartest thing to do now would be to forget this and do the paper on my grandfather instead.

But my curiosity is driving me nuts.

Who is Ned Thump . . . and what is he hiding?

Saturday, Oct. 1

Last night the boss's son sought me out to ask me about my life.

Does he know something?

Does he suspect I am not what I seem?

If he is suspicious, I fear my panicked reaction may have made him even more so.

Is it possible he could have already guessed my secrets?

No, that seems impossible.

On the other hand, there is no doubt a child would be more apt than an adult to figure this out, since children have not yet shut magic out of their lives. I don't worry about this with little Martha. She is so used to me I don't think it would cross her mind. But Cody is different. He doesn't know me as well, and he is curious.

I must be on my guard. The boy may be dangerous.

I hope I will not have to take drastic action.

10/2

Maybe I should actually call this "Cody's Official Weirdness Log," because the stuff going on right now is the main reason I've decided I need a place to write down things I don't particularly want to share with Mr. Liebe.

At first I couldn't decide between "diary" and "journal." "Diary" seemed a little girly, until I did some research (side effect of Mr. Liebe's Biography Project—I research a lot more now) and found that some famous men (Thomas Jefferson! Theodore Roosevelt!) kept diaries. So thinking of that as too girly was kind of dumb.

Even so, I like to be different, so I have decided to call this my Life Log.

I wish now that I hadn't written in my Biography notebook about that horrible night when I upset Granny Aino. This would be the better place for it.

I've also decided this will be the best place to write about Ned, in case he really does have some deep, dark secret.

Anyway, what got me started tonight is that Granny Aino has gone to Florida. She does that every winter, of course. But she left early this year. I don't want to think it's because of me, but I'm afraid that might be the reason.

Not only did it freak her out when I started asking about her past, she looked nervous *every time* I visited after that.

Fortunately, I still have my usual job of watering the plants and feeding Askeladden while Granny is gone. Well, not just feeding him. I'm supposed to spend time every day keeping him company. I don't mind, because I kind of love him. As soon as I sit down he comes galloping over to jump into my lap. Given his size, that's a definite OOOF! moment, but the purring and cuddling that follow make it worth it.

Sometimes Mom and Dad let me stay there overnight so I can watch movies on Gran's ginormous TV. They know the building is safe, and that I can call on Norman the Doorman if there's any problem.

When I do stay over, I get to order takeout. Dang, I love those nights!

But what I need to write about now is this: I did a bad thing when I was over there this afternoon.

I snooped.

I read somewhere that when you snoop in other people's stuff you may find things that upset you, and if that happens, it's only what you deserve.

So I guess I got what I deserved.

Actually, I'm not sure how upset I should be.

Mostly I'm baffled.

Well, baffled and slightly disturbed.

Okay, I should say this first: I have never snooped there before, not once in the three years I've been doing this job. But Gran's weird reaction to my asking about her past really got to me.

That may not be much of an excuse, but it's the truth.

Anyway, in her dining room there's a big piece of furniture called a buffet. The bottom part has two doors with a lot of storage space behind them. Most of that space is filled with china (Granny Aino has a *lot* of plates!) and cardboard boxes crammed full of postcards and junk like that.

This afternoon, for the first time ever, I pulled out some of those boxes to see what was behind them. One thing that looked interesting was a metal box held shut by a latch. I set it aside to look at later, then continued to empty the buffet.

When I had everything out, I noticed a small circular opening in the upper left corner of the buffet's back wall. I stuck in my finger and pulled. A section of the wood came forward by a fraction of an inch. I tried pulling to the left. Nothing happened. But when I pressed to the right, the panel easily slid aside.

Behind it was the dining room wall, as would be expected.

What I wouldn't have expected was that embedded in that wall was a square sheet of metal—iron or steel, I guess—about a foot on each side. In the center of the right side was a red circle about the size of a drink coaster.

The metal didn't appear to be attached to the wall in any way—no bolts or nailheads. Pushed on it. Nothing happened. Tried pulling. It was set so tight in the wall I couldn't even get my fingernails behind it.

The dining room shares that wall with Granny's bedroom. I paced off the distance from the buffet to the door that opens into the hall, then went down the hall and into the bedroom. It looked like the section of wall behind the buffet backed up to her closet.

I opened the closet door. As I did, I heard a sound behind me. Glancing back, I saw Askeladden perched on the end of the bed. He looked . . . well, you can't always read a cat's expression, but I would say he looked annoyed.

The closet floor was covered with laundry. I bent to shift some of it aside and was surprised when my hand struck something solid. Pulling the laundry away, I found a smooth metal cube, about a foot on each side, protruding into the closet.

It looked like a safe. Only I couldn't figure out how you were supposed to open it, since there was no dial or lock or mechanism that I could see.

And why was it way down at floor level, instead of hidden behind a picture on the living room wall, like the safes you see in movies?

Frustrated, I moved the laundry back into place. Then I returned to the dining room and that metal box.

I set it on the table and lifted the lid.

Inside were two things.

One was a metal rod about eight inches long and as thick as my little finger. Tied to it was a label that said, in Finnish, FOR THE CAULDRON.

The other thing was a coil of something dried and leathery. It was kind of gross. At first I didn't want to touch it, but after a moment I took it out and uncoiled it.

Based on the length, the tuft at the end, and last year's school trip to a dairy farm, I'm pretty sure it was a cow's tail.

A leathery, dried-up cow's tail.

What the holy heckenlooper?

Why is my great-grandmother keeping a dried-up cow tail and a metal rod in a metal box at the back of her buffet?

Thursday, Oct. 6

Cody has come to the terminal with his father twice this week. Both times he sought me out, wanting to ask me questions.

I am afraid if I keep refusing him I might lose my job. But can I answer his questions without making him suspicious?

I am also afraid I might lose my temper if he does not stop.

That would not be good.

Very not good.

I have chewed the fingernails on my right hand all the way down to the skin worrying over this.

Text messages between Alex Carhart and Cody Takala

Cody

We're on for the party! Mom was kind of cranky when I got so insistent about coming, but we'll be there.

Alex

I knew I could count on you, Cuz. Been too long since you were here. Aunt Mala's career is doing too well for your own good.

Cody

Hey, watch it. Mom is doing great. Um . . . vow of silence?

Alex

I would rather lose my big toe in a lawn mower accident than spill your secret!

Cody

Mom is doing so well that she's making more than Dad. I think he's mostly okay with it . . . the rent on our apartment is sky-high. But I can tell it bothers him sometimes.

Alex

Totes understand. You should have been here when my dad quit his job last fall. WOWZA!

Cody

Our parents are weird.

Alex

Good thing you and me are so normal.

Cody

HAH!

10/6

I'm afraid I am annoying Ned. I really don't want to be a pest. And I certainly don't want to make him angry. For one thing, he's so big he could probably pop my head like a giant pimple!

(Eeuuuw. Brain pus all over the walls!)

Okay, I'm not really worried about him hurting me. Ned is basically a nice guy. But I'm starting to feel like I'm being mean to him . . . almost like I'm being a bully!

Which is the last thing in the world I want.

I'm going to give it one more try. If Ned still doesn't want to talk, I'll switch back to Grampa.

10/8

This has gotten seriously weird. I mean *seriously.* (As if it wasn't already!) Definitely too weird for the Biography Project notebook I show Mr. Liebe.

So ... last night I tracked Ned down again. When I found him I said, "Please, Ned, I just want to ask you some questions for school!"

Looking down at me (he is SO tall!), he sighed and said, "All right, I will let you ask five questions, as long as they are not about my private life. Is that fair?"

I figured it was better than nothing, so I said yes.

He turned out to be trickier than I expected. His trickiness is not the weird part, but I want to get his answers down while I remember them.

Then I'll write the important part.

Q&A

Me: Why don't you want to answer questions?

Ned: Because I am a very private person. Talking about my personal life makes me uncomfortable.

Me: I'm sorry. I'll stop now if you want. (Note: I really did mean that!)

Ned: No, I agreed to answer five questions, and you agreed that after that you would leave me alone. So ask your next question.

Me: Where do you live?

Ned: Let's simply say I am a convenient distance from work.

Me: Ned!

Ned: I said I would not answer questions about my personal life. That was personal.

Me: Okay, do I get another?

Ned: No. And that was your third question.

I wanted to scream. But I also wanted to ask a really good one, since I had run through most of my chances. Finally, I came up with one that I thought might work:

Me: What should I know about you that I don't?

Ned: (after a long delay) I am stranger than you think, and I have a tragic history.

Me: Are you really going to stop there?

Ned: Yes. And that was your fifth question.

Okay, so that made me want to scream even more.

But now comes the really important (and really weird) part. Speaking slowly, Ned said, "Cody, it is not that I do not like you. But I am shy, and being interviewed makes me uncomfortable. I promised to answer five questions and I have done that, even if you didn't like the answers. So do you promise that this is done now?"

I sighed and said, "I promise."

"Then let's shake on it," said Ned.

He held out his hand. It was almost the size of a tennis racket.

I extended my own, which disappeared inside his massive grip. As his fingers closed around mine, a weird shock jolted up my arm. I don't mean some little static electricity shock. I felt as if I had grabbed a live wire!

I knew Ned felt it, too, because he gasped, then let go of my hand and backed away, looking frightened.

"What was *that*?" I asked, shaking my arm, which was still tingling.

"I don't know," answered Ned, staring at his hand as if he'd never seen it before.

Then he turned and ran.

I did the same, in the opposite direction.

Saturday, Oct. 8

I could not sleep today because I am so troubled by what happened with Cody last night.

I agreed, perhaps foolishly, to let him ask me five questions. I did this in the hope that it would put an end to his pestering.

I'll admit I played a bit sharply with the boy, counting everything he asked as one of his allotted questions, even if they were things he clearly did not mean to be part of the interview. But that's the way it works in the Enchanted Realm! However, it's also probably why I did answer one question with more information than I should have. I was feeling a bit guilty about the other ones.

But that's not the real issue.

The real issue is that when we shook hands at the end of the interview, a powerful jolt of energy—sudden, unexpected, and unlike anything I've ever felt before—passed between us.

What in the world could it mean?

What could have caused it?

I hope the boy is all right. Part of me thinks I should check with his father to see. But if Cody *is* all right, and hasn't said anything to his father, then going to Mr. Takala would just create new problems.

Wish I had someone to consult with about this.

Feel more alone than usual.

10/8 (night)

If I thought things were weird before, they're triple weird now.

That's because I just had a conversation with a cat.

Askeladden, to be specific.

This is hard to write, because my hands are shaking.

If anyone else reads this, they'll think I've lost my mind.

And I can't *talk* to anyone about it because they would think I was just skying!

Good grief! I just realized my real life has gotten more bizarre than my made-up stories!

Deep breath. Okay, after I finished writing about my encounter with Ned, I walked over to Granny Aino's apartment to do my job.

As usual, Askeladden was lounging on the couch, curled in a silvery-gray cat Q. Normally he just dozes—or pretends to doze—until I sit down and pat my lap. But this afternoon I had gone only a few steps into the apartment when he leaped to his feet. Tail frizzing out, back arched, he stared at me and hissed.

Then he said, "What in the world has happened to you?"

Seriously, he *said* it.

Out loud!

Actually, what came out of his mouth was a mixture of yowls and yips.

But I understood every one of them!

"Did you just talk to me?" I asked. Which was kind of dumb, since I knew that was exactly what had just happened.

I don't think I was shaping my words any differently. Even so, it was clear Askeladden understood them, because he said, "Yes, I talked to you. The question is, why did you understand me?"

"I don't have the slightest idea!"

Askeladden jumped off the couch, walked to where I was standing, and began sniffing around me. Finally he said, "Pick me up!"

I bent and scooped him into my arms, feeling a bit silly for taking orders from a cat. He sniffed at my hands, and his eyes grew wide. "Have you been talking to a troll?" he demanded.

"Of course not!"

"Are you certain?"

My own eyes grew wide as I thought about my conversation with Ned last night . . . thought about his enormous size . . . and that jolting handshake.

OMG! Is it possible Ned Thump is a troll?

No, come on, Cody. That's absurd.

But there I was, talking to a cat.

So who am I to judge what's absurd?

Askeladden continued to stare at me. "You sure you haven't been talking to a troll?"

"Trolls aren't real."

"Yeah, and neither are talking cats. But here you are talking to me. So either you've gone nuts, or something very strange is going on."

"All right, let's say I did talk to a troll. What would that have to do with being able to talk to you?"

"I'm not sure I should say. Maybe you should talk to your grandfather."

"What would Grampa know about this?"

"Not him. Your *other* grandfather."

"Are you serious? I've never talked to Raimo in my life. My family is pretty much not speaking to him."

"Well, maybe it's time you started."

"I wouldn't even know how to reach him."

"Then maybe you should do a little more snooping."

I blushed, thinking about how Askeladden had watched me the last time I did that. But I also thought about what I'd found and realized I could ask him about it now.

"Why is Granny keeping a dried-up cow tail in a metal box?"

"Talk to your grandfather," repeated the cat.

"How?"

Askeladden sighed and said, "Really, Cody, do I have to tell you everything? All right, you'll find his cell number in the desk over there. He's in Finland, so given the time difference, you should probably just text him."

He shook his head, then curled up and went back to sleep.

A NOTE ON
THE NATURE OF MAGIC

From *The Sayings of Granny Squannit*
Collected by Weegun of the Makiaweesug

The answer to your problem may be closer at hand than you think. This is not a matter of coincidence. It is in the very nature of magic that magical things tend to draw together.

However, you cannot take this for granted.

Nor can you count on magic doing all the work.

Open your eyes and ask questions!

Sunday, Oct. 9

Something is changing.
I don't know what it is.
I don't know why it is.
But I do know *that* it is.
I am twitching with nerves.
I am positive it has something to do with the boy.

Text message from Cody Takala to Raimo Takala

Cody

Hi, Grampa! I know we've never talked, and I hope I'm not bothering you. But I found your cell number in Granny Aino's desk and I really need your advice. Could you get back to me, please?

10/15

And . . . the weirdness just keeps on coming!

Friday night I was hoping to track down Ned to see if I could figure out *something* about what was going on. Instead Mom told me I had to stay home and get to bed "at a reasonable hour" so we could get an early start on our trip out to Connecticut for Destiny's birthday party.

Since I was the one who had made a fuss about going to begin with, and Mom had turned down a major gig when I guilted her about family ties, I was totally busted on that.

Besides, I really did want to go. I like Aunt Ellen and Uncle Dennis, and I really, really like my cousins, Bennett, Alex, and Destiny. Ben is a few years older than me, and a super soccer player—though according to Mom he went through an odd phase last year when he quit soccer to be a poet. She says he's back to normal now.

Alex is about my age, and we get along really well. One thing I love about her is that she's a total slob, which means the mess in her room *always* makes my room look good by comparison. This is very useful when I am having conversations with my mother about whether I need to clean up more.

Also, we swap books a lot, which is why I brought my backpack with me.

Which turned out to be a good thing.

I think.

As for the birthday girl, Destiny is only in first grade. But she's totally cute and always makes me laugh.

When we go out there, I mostly like to hang with Bennett. I don't want to seem like a tagalong, of course, but Ben is usually cool about it, even though he's older than me. But after Destiny's party he took off with some friends, leaving me to sit in Alex's room and talk with her.

From the moment I went in, two things struck me as strange.

First, except for her desk, which was covered with its normal mess, the room was neat and tidy. Given the way Al's room usually looks, even if she has supposedly "cleaned up for company," this was startling.

Shocking, even.

Second, she had a huge pink Barbie dollhouse. The front of it was facing the wall. The back—the part that's open so you can move stuff around in it—was covered with a sheet.

"I thought you told me you were done with Barbies," I said, pointing to the pink monstrosity.

Blushing a little, she said, "I have that out for an art project!"

I've seen some of Alex's other art, so this made sense. She does some pretty strange projects.

We talked about school for a while, and then I had to use the bathroom. When I came back Alex had an odd look on her face.

"What's wrong?" I asked.

"I'm not sure. There's someone here who wants to meet you."

"Who?" I asked, looking around. "Where?"

"I'll explain after you make an I-hope-to-die-a-death-so-horrible-it-curls-your-toes-if-I-dare-tell-anyone-about-this oath."

Al and I had started making this kind of promise when we were little kids and wanted to swear each other to secrecy. Mostly we used it when one of us broke a window or something. The person challenged to make the oath has to come up with a new and totally horrifying way to die if he or she breaks it.

"Lick your thumb and make a spit swear," Alex said urgently.

Still looking at her like she was nuts, I licked my thumb, held it out, and said, "I promise to keep this a secret, and if I break that promise may a ravenous griffin tear open my belly and eat my living guts while I scream in misery."

Alex nodded in satisfaction and pressed her thumb

against mine. Then she took a deep breath and said, "Come on out, Angus."

I looked behind me, toward her closet, wondering if she had a friend hiding there for some reason.

Alex tapped me on the shoulder and pointed in the other direction, toward the dollhouse.

I lurched back in shock when I saw a small hand draw back the sheet.

Then a small man—small as in, *about twelve inches tall!*—stepped out.

Alex clapped her hand over my mouth to stifle my squawk.

Clearly, she had been expecting my reaction.

I probably would have been even more freaked out, except the handshake with Ned, and the fact that I was now talking to my great-grandmother's cat, had already made it clear the world was far stranger than I had thought.

Even so, I was pretty boggled.

Speaking in a formal tone, Alex said, "Angus, this is my cousin, Cody Takala. Cody, this is Angus Cairns." She paused, then added, "He's a brownie."

I shook my head like a dog that's just climbed out of the water. I'm not sure why I did that . . . trying to get the world to make sense again, I guess.

"Pleased to meet you, Cody," said the brownie. He spoke with a strong accent. Later I realized it was Scottish.

"Um . . . pleased to meet you, too," I said. I wondered if I should try to shake his hand, then realized the idea was ridiculous, since his hand was about the size of a marble.

"So what is this about, Angus?" asked Alex. She sounded confused and worried. Turning to me, she added, "Ben and Destiny know about Angus, but other than that he is a total secret."

Putting his hands on his hips, the brownie looked up at me and said, "You've been puttering about with magic, lad. I can sense it on you, and I want to know what it's about." Narrowing his eyes, he said, "Have you been to the Enchanted Realm?"

"What's the Enchanted Realm?" I asked.

"It's where the magical people live," said Alex.

"Huh?" was my brilliant response.

"You know! Brownies and goblins and mermaids. That kind of thing."

"I am nae a *thing*!" Angus snapped.

"Sorry," said Alex. Turning back to me, she added, "Also magical creatures. You know . . . unicorns, griffins, dragons, and so on."

I couldn't tell her that was stupid while I was staring at a guy who was only twelve inches tall.

"Talk, boy!" Angus said. "What is happening with you? I hope you appreciate I'm takin' a risk showing myself this way. But I fear you may be getting yourself in over your head. So . . . what have you been messing about with?"

I told them about shaking hands with Ned, and being able to talk to Askeladden. I half expected Alex to laugh, but I guess the fact that she had a brownie living in her dollhouse made it easier to accept things like this.

As for Angus, he squinched up his face, then said, "Alex, could you fetch Bubbles?"

Bubbles is their family cat. He is big (though not as big as Askeladden), orange, and usually pretty surly.

"Be right back," Alex said.

While she was gone I took a closer look at Angus. The little man appeared to be about as old as my dad. (Alex told me later that he's actually one hundred and fifty!) He had thick, curly brown hair, a pointy nose, and large ears that were even more pointy. He wore a red coat, brown pants, and boots that curled up at the toes.

"So . . . what are you thinking this is all about?" I asked.

"I don't know, I'm still gathering information. Now be quiet and let me think."

A few minutes later Alex returned with Bubbles and deposited him on the floor in front of me. The cat took one look at me, arched his back, and said, "What in the world has happened to you?"

"That's what we're trying to find out," I answered.

"Cody, are you talking to my cat?" asked Alex, her eyes wide.

"Indeed he is," said Angus. He bit his lip and began to pace back and forth in front of the dollhouse. Finally, he stopped and said, "Alex, I know 'tis you to whom I am assigned. But this lad is family, and I fear he's got himself mixed up in something he canna understand. I think I should investigate. But I need your permission to do so."

"Permission granted," said Alex.

Angus returned to the closet. After a few minutes he came back out wearing a backpack that was like a miniature version of my own. He was clutching something that looked like a tent peg.

"Do you think you'll need that?" asked Alex.

"Might," said the brownie.

"What is it?" I asked.

"Rather not say right now," Angus replicd. "I'll only be using it in case of extreme need."

That was annoying, but I could tell I wasn't going to get anything more out of him. And I was already in such a state of shock that I didn't think I could absorb anything more anyway.

When Mom called upstairs to say it was time to go, we carefully settled Angus and his pack (and the peg) in my own backpack.

Which is why there is, at this very minute, a brownie

busily making a comfortable hiding place for himself in my closet.

I would like to write, "I don't think my life can get any weirder." But I'm afraid if I did, it would just be an invitation for the world to prove me wrong.

Monday night Angus and I plan to go in search of Ned.

I am excited . . . and slightly terrified.

Text messages between Alex Carhart and Cody Takala

Alex

I didn't want to say this in front of Angus, but I think I should warn you that he has a bit of a temper.

Cody

At this point a cranky brownie is the least of my worries. But I appreciate the heads-up!

Alex

He's really very sweet. Just grouchy.

Cody

I'm feeling the same way myself right now!

Text messages between Cody Takala and Raimo Takala

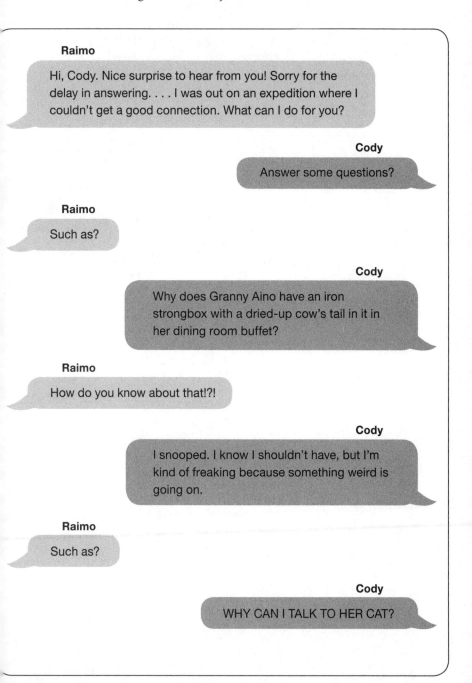

Raimo

Hi, Cody. Nice surprise to hear from you! Sorry for the delay in answering. . . . I was out on an expedition where I couldn't get a good connection. What can I do for you?

Cody

Answer some questions?

Raimo

Such as?

Cody

Why does Granny Aino have an iron strongbox with a dried-up cow's tail in it in her dining room buffet?

Raimo

How do you know about that!?!

Cody

I snooped. I know I shouldn't have, but I'm kind of freaking because something weird is going on.

Raimo

Such as?

Cody

WHY CAN I TALK TO HER CAT?

Raimo

Cody, I need to stop this conversation right here. I am going to get in touch with your great-grandmother. If she wants to tell you any more, she can. I am sorry I have not been a better grandfather. Things in our family are . . . a mess.

Cody

A mess how?

Cody

Grampa?

Cody

GRAMPA???

10/16

What in the world is going on with this family?
What is going on with me?
And what does Ned Thump have to do with it?
I feel like I'm losing my mind.
Except I think it's the people around me who are crazy.

10/17

I'm writing this in Dad's office at GCT. In a little while Angus and I are going out to look for Ned.

I wonder what will happen when Ned meets a brownie. If Ned really is just a very big human being—and I have to keep in mind that that's possible, even if it no longer seems likely—he might totally freak out.

However he reacts, their meeting will be strange to see, since Ned is so big and Angus so small.

But that's not what I want to get on paper right now, which is the thing I discovered this afternoon.

The fact that Ned's name seems so oddly familiar to me has been bugging me more and more since that electrifying handshake. So today I did what I should have thought of doing before, and went plunging through Grampa Raimo's collections of Scandinavian tales.

And there it was . . . "The Tale of Nettie Thump"!

Mom read that story to me when I was little. I didn't like it, because it was so sad, so it wasn't one I asked her to repeat. But this afternoon I used her scanner to make a copy of it. I've stashed it in the folder where I'm keeping notes about what's going on.

Is it possible Ned is connected to that old story?

Wouldn't it be weird if Nettie was his mother or something?

How long do trolls live, anyway?

Can't write more now. Dad just went out to do his rounds.

Angus is looking at me and tapping his foot.

Time to go on a Ned hunt!

Tuesday, Oct. 18

I have been discovered . . . and in a way far stranger than I had expected.

It was Cody, of course. From the time he began trying to question me, I feared something like this might happen.

Well, I feared he might uncover the secret that I am a troll. It never occurred to me he would uncover *both* my secrets!

✦　✦　✦

Had to take a break and walk around my cave several times to calm myself before I could write more.

So . . . here is what happened. Last night as I was making my rounds, simply trying to do my job, Cody approached me again.

"What do you want?" I asked.

At the same time, I clasped my hands behind my back so he could not try to sneak in another shake. I tried not to sound angry—it would not be good to frighten the boss's son—but the truth is I was very unhappy to see him.

"I need to talk to you," he replied. "It's important."

"Can't you leave me alone?" I pleaded.

Cody shook his head. "Something strange has happened. It involves you, and I'm trying to understand it."

The boy sounded so desperate I couldn't bring myself to deny him, much as I wanted to. With a sigh, I said, "What's happened?"

"I can talk to animals!"

A bizarre thought crossed my mind.

I pushed it away, thinking it couldn't be true.

"Well, at least to cats," he continued. "I haven't tried anything else. I'm kind of afraid to. If I can talk to cows, I'll never be able to eat another hamburger!"

"I suspect it will be just cats," I said, hoping that would reassure him.

Unfortunately, that was not the end of it.

"Ned, I'm sure shaking hands with you caused this. I need to know why. But before we talk any more I have to introduce you to someone."

Cody knelt, took off his backpack, opened the top, and said, "Come on out, Angus."

From the pack stepped a manlike being no more than a foot high. He was like a tiny version of a tonttu, but without the beard.

Gesturing between the two of us, Cody said, "Angus Cairns, meet Ned Thump. Ned Thump, this is Angus Cairns."

"What are you?" I asked.

"A brownie!" cried the little man, as if he was offended

that I did not know this. "A brownie through and through. And you . . . what are you, ya great lumbering thing? You're clearly nae a human!"

A shudder rippled through me. My disguise had been pierced in front of the boy! Clearly this "brownie" (whatever that is) was from the Enchanted Realm. Just as clearly, he sensed that I was, too, because the next thing he said was "What are you doing in the human world? Do you live here?"

I am nearly seven feet tall. So I should not have been made nervous by someone I could squash with one stomp of my foot. But something about this "brownie" was compelling. It was more than the force of his personality (which was enormous for someone so small). It was this: after keeping the secret of being from the Enchanted Realm for so very, very long, it felt unexpectedly good to have someone recognize me for what I really am. (Though, of course, at this point he had only discovered the first of my secrets.)

"I am in exile," I said. "And why are *you* here? Clearly you do not belong in the human world any more than I do."

"My presence is due to an old family curse. Well, the curse was what brought me here. Now I have family ties that I value."

This puzzled me. *Can an Enchanted have close relations with a human???*

Cody spoke up, saying, "Angus lives with my cousin Alex. I met him this weekend when I went out to visit her. He sensed that something strange had happened to me."

"I sensed something of the Realm on the boy," added the brownie. "Something that shouldn't have been there. He thinks it has to do with a handshake you've shared, but this baffles me. What could a mere handshake have to do with anything?"

"I don't know," I answered, with complete honesty.

"Well, what are you, exactly?" persisted the brownie.

I sighed. Then, since there was nothing to be gained by denying it, I said, "I am a troll."

"I knew it!" cried Cody. Then, to my utter astonishment, he said, "Are you any relation to Nettie Thump?"

I staggered back. Before I could stop it, my traitorous tongue undid me.

"I *am* Nettie Thump!" I blurted.

Cody stared at me in amazement. "You're a girl?" he cried.

I nodded. As I did, a huge surge of emotion swelled within me. I felt as if I were going to cry . . . which is impossible, of course.

But I almost wished that I could.

I have been hiding for so very long. . . .

10/18

OMG . . . Ned Thump is a girl!!!

Or a woman.

Or a "troll-hag." Which seems like a really cruel thing to call her, but it's what he . . . I mean *she* . . . insists is the correct term.

This all came out last night when Angus and I tracked her down. When I asked about "The Tale of Nettie Thump," Ned (which was what I thought he should be called at that point) said it was her story!

I mean *his*.

Seriously—Ned Thump is not only a troll, he's a female!

I mean *she's* a female.

(This is hard to write without getting my pronouns mixed up!)

Even with that discovery, we still don't know what that jolting handshake was all about. Well, Nettie has a theory. But it's so bizarre I can't bring myself to write it down.

I wish Alex was here. I could use someone who's dealt with magical stuff to talk to. I could text her, but that's not the same as having a face-to-face brainstorming session to figure this out.

I would talk to Angus about the situation, but he's sleeping right now. (He made a cubby for himself out of a shoe box, which I stashed on the top shelf in my closet.)

I'm getting to like the little guy, despite his temper. He's been telling me about the Enchanted Realm. What he says is fascinating, but also mind-boggling. I wouldn't believe it, if it wasn't coming from a pointy-eared little man who's only twelve inches tall.

I think the thing to do right now is reread "The Tale of Nettie Thump."

Also, I need to have another talk with Grampa Raimo.

The Tale of Nettie Thump

From *Secret Stories of Scandinavia*

Collected by Raimo Takala

Once upon a time, and what a time it was, there lived a troll whose name was Nettie Thump. She was not as tall as a tree, nor as wide as a barn door, and her nose was not quite as big as a potato. But she was big enough overall, and ugly enough, too, as well a troll might be.

Nettie's father was the King of Troll Mountain. Her mother, Hekthema, was the Witch Queen of that same place, and it was her dearest wish that Nettie should marry a human prince and drag him down to the troll world, where they could make sport of him.

One dark night Hekthema used her troll magic to cast a glamour over her daughter. When it was done Nettie seemed as beautiful as a sunrise, as delicate as thistledown, and as fragrant as lily of the valley . . . a lovely flower well known for its poisonous properties.

The enchantment in place, Hekthema set her troll-girl

on a path known to be followed by the prince, wrenched her ankle for her, then left her there, seeming beautiful and helpless, to catch the eye of the prince as he passed by.

He did not come for two days, during which time Nettie was given no food or water, and so became—to human eye—even more pale and needful. Meanwhile Hekthema, hiding in the nearby bushes, grew ever more impatient. She would pull her daughter's hair and pinch her daughter's side, but what was the troll-girl to do if the prince passed not by?

Finally, on the third day, the prince, whose name was Gustav Fredrik, came riding along the path. When Nettie saw him approach she began to sob, as she had been ordered. There were no actual tears, of course, because trolls cannot weep. But she made a good show of it.

When the prince spotted Nettie, who truly was in deep distress, he stopped to help her, as would any genuine prince.

"Why, miss," he said, in gentle tones, "what troubles you so that you weep here beside the road?"

And Nettie replied, as she had been instructed, "Oh, I am a maiden all forlorn. The man I loved has turned against me, and when I fled his wrath I twisted my ankle. He laughed when he saw that, and left me here alone and sorrowful."

These words went straight to the prince's heart. He offered Nettie food and drink, and said that he would lead her home.

"No, no," she said. "My home is nearby, and I can limp my way there. But first I must finish my mourning, for my heart is sore and shamed."

Then she thanked him for the food, and blessed him for the drink, and said that if he was willing, she would meet him there the next day.

To this the prince happily agreed.

When Gustav Fredrik was gone, Nettie's mother grabbed her hair and twisted it into a knot, then hissed in her ear, "That was well enough done. Even more well done must it be on the morrow."

Then she beat Nettie about the shoulders so that bruises bloomed on what seemed to be smooth and slender flesh—though in truth the troll-girl's shoulders were wide as a door and thick with muscle.

On the next evening Nettie sat once more in sorrow.

When the prince came riding by he said, "Why, miss, what troubles you today that you once more sit so forlorn beside the road?"

"Oh, the man who was to be my love returned. When I said I would no more with him go, he beat me about the shoulders, and now here I sit, lost and lorn, weary and worn, and much afilled with fear."

"If I can but catch this man who is no more than a beast, I will teach him some manners!" cried the prince. "In the meantime, let me treat your purple bruises."

From his pack he pulled a potion, which he rubbed upon her shoulders. His touch was firm, his fingers fair, and in Nettie's heart a warmth was born.

When he was gone, Nettie's mother grabbed her hair and twisted it into a knot, then hissed in her ear, "That was well enough done. Even more well done must it be on the morrow."

And that night she boxed the troll-lass about the ears, till angry welts bloomed on what seemed to be snow-white cheeks—though in truth they were coarse as tree bark and tough as leather.

On the next day Nettie sat once more in sorrow.

When the prince rode by, he said, "Why, miss, what troubles you so today that you once more sit so forlorn beside the road?"

A third time hiding her falseness, Nettie said, "The man who was to be my love came back again last night. But when I said I would no more with him go, he cruelly pinched my cheeks till they flamed. So now I sit, lost and weary, sad and dreary, and much afire with fear."

"Let me but catch this man who is lower than a toad and less than a gnat, and I will teach him some proper manners!" cried the prince. "In the meantime, let me soothe your silken cheeks."

From his pack he pulled an ointment, which he daubed upon her fiery face. His touch was firm, his fingers fair, and in Nettie's heart the warmth became a fire.

"Now come with me and be my bride," said the prince to Nettie. "You are lovelier by far than all the maids my mother has presented, and I would have you to wife. I want you to be the one who sits by my side when I am king."

In the brush behind the bride, Hekthema rubbed her hands with glee. She knew that if this came to pass, her husband, the King of Troll Mountain, would be well pleased.

So off went Nettie with the handsome prince, his winsome bride to be. But in her heart now burned two flames. One flame was a torch of longing, for she ached to be his bride in truth, and carry him to the world below the mountain, where he would be hers forever. But the other flame was not of desire. Rather it was of true love, and she felt singed with shame at the idea that she should betray the prince when he had been so kind to her.

For kindness was something new to Nettie Thump.

When the prince presented the beautiful-seeming lass at court, the king and queen gave her warm welcome, and quickly approved the marriage. Oddly, as the prince continued to treat her with tender kindness, Nettie grew increasingly unhappy. This was because as the flame of love grew ever stronger, it pained her ever more deeply to know that if she wed the prince she would draw him to his doom.

At last she decided that this she could not do, and there was nothing for it but to tell him the truth. So on the night before the wedding she asked the prince if he would walk a way with her.

"Of course, my love," he said.

Then Nettie led him to the place where he had first seen her. There, in the moonlight, she said, "My prince, I must show you the truth."

With a single word she dropped the glamour that Hekthema had put upon her.

When Gustav Fredrik saw her true face, and her great size, and realized she was a troll, he turned and fled in horror.

With breaking heart, Nettie watched him go. In that moment of truth she had lost not only her prince but also her world. For after what she had done, she could no more return to the world under the mountain. Her mother's fury would be fiery, and her father's rage like that of a volcano. Who ever heard of a troll falling in love with a prince?

So it was that Nettie Thump wandered off the mountain, and out of her own story, and has never been heard of since.

Now Rippitty Rappitty Rover,
It's time this story's over!

Wednesday, Oct. 19

I have kept my twin secrets for nearly one hundred and fifty years. Now along comes this boy who in a matter of days pulls both of them out of me.

Part of me is relieved. It feels good not to be hiding anymore!

Well, it would feel good, except another part of me is in a total state of fret. What if Cody tells his father about me?

No, I don't think he would do that.

Yet I cannot help but worry.

Pah. I'm being foolish! Not only would Cody never tell his father, if he did, his father would never believe him.

Even so, being revealed to the boy this way has shaken me badly.

10/19

Reading Nettie's story made me really angry. It's bad enough when people get bullied by others their own age. Nettie was bullied by her own *parents*. How rotten is that?!

It's weird to think of someone as big as Nettie getting bullied, but I guess it happens. We had a guest speaker at school last year to talk about bullies. She quoted a poem that went:

> *Big fleas have little fleas*
> *Upon their backs to bite 'em;*
> *And little fleas have smaller fleas,*
> *And so on, ad infinitum*

(*Ad infinitum* is Latin for "forever.")

Then she said that the same thing was true for bullies:

> *Big bullies have bigger ones*
> *To push 'em all about,*

And bigger ones have bigger still,
Till time and time run out.

Not that Nettie was ever a bully.
But, dang, her mother sure was.
Makes me angry.

October 17

Dear Cody,

This is difficult to write. But after hearing from your Grampa Raimo about what is happening, I decided it was important to tell you the truth about your heritage.

Let me say up front that I know you were puzzled and hurt by the way I reacted when you wanted to ask about our family history.

It is a story more unusual than you might expect.

Your Grampa Raimo knows the truth. Its impact on him is the main reason he returned to Finland so many years ago.

Your father does not, largely because the secret story of our family has not affected him the same way. He was only mildly curious about our past, and much more interested in the here and now of his own life.

No blame in that. It is the way of some children. And though your Grampa Raimo and I both grieve the separation between him and your father, we also agree that it is probably just as well.

You, however, are different, which I have suspected from the time you were little. Different not only in your curiosity, but also in the way the traits that are part of your blood heritage were showing up. I saw it in your affinity for animals, and in your tendency to "sky," as you like to put it.

In those ways, you are much more like your grandfather than your father.

Enclosed with this letter is a translation of some pages from your great-grandfather's journal, written many decades ago.

I'm sorry you never had a chance to know him. He was an amazing man. He was only in his late teens when he wrote these pages . . . a farm boy with little sense of the world, and no sense at all of what he was about to fall into.

The girl in the story is me, of course . . . me long, long ago.

Cody, I am truly sorry for any distress I have caused you. I love you with all my heart, and I hope that when you read these pages you will understand why I was so reluctant to talk about my past.

What you will find here will likely leave you with many questions.

I have given your Grampa Raimo permission to answer anything you might ask.

With all my love,
Great-Granny Aino

April 12

While passing through the woods today as I was walking from our farm to the village, I met the most beautiful girl I have ever seen. She was sitting on a fallen tree beside the path, singing a wordless tune while she combed her hair. Though the melody was one I did not know, it seemed to go straight to my heart.

I stopped to listen. In truth, I don't think I could have walked on even had I wanted to. After a time she looked up at me, and it was all I could do to keep breathing, for she was like a dream come alive, with golden hair and eyes the color of the sky on a clear sunny day.

"Can I help you?" she asked, and I heard a hint of laughter in her voice.

I nearly blurted out, "Yes, just let me stand here and look at you." Fortunately, I managed to choke those words back, and said instead, "Can you tell me the words that go to your song?"

"There are no words," says she, standing. "And you were not meant to hear it anyway. I had best go before I get in trouble."

And with that she began to back away.

"Wait!" I cried. "I want to talk to you!"

She smiled and said, "Not today. No, not today. But maybe soon. Do you pass this way often?"

"But once a week," I replied sadly, wishing that I could say, "Every day!" Alas, my duties at the farm do not allow for that.

"Well, I will be here next week, if I can," she said, still backing away.

"Do you promise?" I asked.

"If I can," she repeated with a laugh.

Then she ducked behind a tree. I waited to see her walk on, but there was no sign of her. After several moments I walked to the tree, thinking she was hiding there.

She was nowhere to be seen!

April 14

I cannot stop thinking about the girl in the forest.

April 15

I hope so much that she will be there when next I go to the village.

April 19

I saw her again today! And talked to her!

The odd thing is, I can't really remember anything she said. I only know that I was happy being with her.

I cannot wait until next week, when I hope to see her again.

April 20

The days drag by. Will Saturday never get here?

April 21

Not a good day. Mother has noticed how I am moping and mooning about, and she finally got the story out of me.

"Beware of strange maidens you meet in the wood," she said sternly. "Are you sure she's even human?"

That put a bit of a scare into me. The girl's beauty is so great it is almost unearthly, and I certainly feel as if I have been enchanted. But I am well entrapped, and the longing to see her grows greater by the day.

April 22

Today Mother summoned Grandmother to come talk to me. Grandmother is the oldest and wisest woman I know, and I am certain she is speaking good sense when she says I should avoid the girl.

Why will my heart not listen?

Seeing that I was deaf to her advice, she took a puff on her pipe, then let out the smoke and said, "Boy, do but this one thing. Ask this girl of yours to spin three times about. If she will not, promise me you will never see her again. If she agrees, then see what you will see."

It seemed the strangest request, but I can find no harm in it. Out of respect for my grandmother, whom I honor above all others in the world, I will do this thing.

April 26

My heart is seized with sorrow, and a touch of anger. As I was heading to town today, my girl (in my heart, she is my girl still, though I do not know if I will ever see her again) was waiting in the usual spot, combing her golden hair and singing a song that could melt a heart of stone.

"May I sit beside you?" I asked.

She smiled and nodded, and I took my place beside her

on the fallen tree. At once I was nearly drunk on the scent of her, which was as if she had bathed in blossoms of lily of the valley.

As she continued to comb her golden hair I said, "May I know your name?"

"I am called Aino," she replied.

Somehow it felt like a great gift.

Gathering my courage, I said, "I have another request."

"And what would that be?" she asked with a smile.

"Would you stand and turn three times about for me?"

Aino leaped to her feet and backed away. "Why do you ask that?" she shrieked. *"Why do you ask that?"*

Then she turned and fled.

I felt a total brute.

As she turned, I noticed an odd hollow in her back, where her blouse caved in . . . as if there was nothing there. It made me shudder.

What does this mean?

Will I ever see her again?

Do I even want to see her again?

Yes, of course! Though it would mean breaking my promise to my grandmother, I cannot get the girl out of my mind.

Still, a strange fear troubles my heart.

What does Grandmother suspect that I do not?

Why did she tell me to ask this of the girl?

April 29

I have not slept for the last three nights. All I do is toss and turn, and reach out for someone who is not there.

Will she be at the fallen tree on Saturday?

Or have I lost her forever?

May 3

Yesterday was a day of horror and delight.

I set off for the village filled with a mixture of hope and dread.

Even before I could see the fallen tree, I heard her singing! At the first note, my heart leapt with joy.

As I rounded the bend that led to our meeting place, I saw that she was standing, rather than sitting on the tree as was her normal way.

"You are here!" I cried, unable to hide my joy.

"Where else would I be?" she answered. Then, her face serious, she said, "Do you still want me to turn three times about?"

I closed my eyes and thought. I was terrified that if I said yes, she would once again flee. But I also knew that my grandmother would not have told me to ask this if it had not been important.

Finally, I said, "Only if you are willing."

She looked at me for a moment, then nodded. Her voice solemn as a preacher's, she said, "That is the best answer. And for you, I am willing."

In those words I heard so much trust and love that it pierced my heart as much as ever her beauty had.

As I watched, she turned about once, twice, three times.

On the third turn, I cried out in shock when I saw the tip of a tail drop beneath the hem of her dress. She must have had it bound up, but it had come loose in the turning. In that moment I realized what Grandmother had suspected all along.

The girl was huldra!

Horrified, I turned to flee.

"Wait!" she cried.

I could not help myself. I turned back to her. My heart nearly stopped when she held out her arms, welcoming me to her embrace.

"I cannot," I said. "I cannot go with you to your underground world."

"Did I ask that?" she replied gently.

"Then what do you want?" I said, confused.

"If you will have me, I will come with you to your Christian church to be married. But we will need a faithful bridesmaid, for when we say our vows my tail will fall off, and it must be quickly hidden. The hollow in my back, which is like that in a dead tree, will disappear. In that moment, I will become fully human. But you must know, my love, that my beauty will not last. It will fade over the years, far more rapidly than for most women, until I am like unto a crone. But in exchange for that loss of beauty, you will have the most faithful and loving wife that ever man could ask for.

"I know, dear man, that I am honey to your eyes, music to your ears, silk to your fingertips. But that will go, it will go. In the end, I will be only an old and ugly woman who loves you with all her heart and cares for you with all her strength. Can you live with that? Can you want that?"

I stood frozen for a very long time, my heart at war with itself.

Then a kind of peace came over me as I realized what my heart most truly desired, which was not the beauty of her face, but the warmth of her love, the love that had given her the courage to reveal her truth to me.

I reached out my arms. She ran to them.

For the first time, I held her.

For the first time, I kissed her.

I felt the hollow in her back as I put my arms around her, but I did not let it bother me.

Next week, we will be wed.

I am alight with joy. But it is a joy tempered with fear, for we know the troll world will not easily let her go.

Fortunately, we have a plan.

A desperate one, it is true, but I have hope it will work.

My bride-to-be is not only beautiful, she is incredibly brave, and if she can manage to escape with her family's magic cauldron, all might yet be well.

Mother does not approve of the plan and fears it will fail.

Grandmother is encouraging.

As for me, I can hardly stay in my skin.

May 12

It worked! We are in America!

And so our new life begins, far from the world of the trolls.

I shall miss Finland.

Even so, I consider myself the luckiest man in the world.

From: C-Tak@kid2kid.com
To: R.Takala@finnet.fn
Date: 10/19
Subject: NEED HELP!

Dear Grampa,

I need someone to talk to, and it looks like you're it.

I did as you suggested and contacted Granny Aino. So unless she is crazy—and I don't think she is—I now know the truth. If I understand this correctly, you are half huldra, Dad is a quarter huldra, and I am one-eighth huldra.

What the heck is "huldra"?

How come no one told me any of this before?

And what does it mean for me?

Now here's something you don't know! As near as I can figure out, the reason I can talk to cats is that last week I shook hands with a troll! I mean it. A genuine troll! I didn't know she was a troll at the time, but I figured it out a couple of nights ago.

And here's what might really surprise you. The troll I am talking about is Nettie Thump . . . the same Nettie Thump who is in that story in one of your books! She's pretending to be a human, and a guy, and she works for Dad at Grand Central.

But I still don't understand why shaking hands with Nettie made it possible for me to talk to cats.

Please, Grampa, can you explain any of this?

Love,

Cody

From: R.Takala@finnet.fn
To: C-Tak@kid2kid.com
Date: 10/19
Subject: Re: NEED HELP!

Dear Cody,

There's a lot here to respond to, and you certainly do deserve a response. Not to mention a heartfelt apology, which I hereby offer.

Just so you'll know, the reason your great-grandmother and I didn't tell you about all this is that we never imagined it would affect you. You are, after all, only one-eighth huldra. And since your dad never displayed signs of the bloodline showing up, we figured it was fading with each generation.

I suppose I should have had a hint that your huldra genes might be dominant when your great-grandmother told me about your "skying," since a gift for storytelling is one of the benefits of being of huldra descent. But even if I had wondered about that, I would never have guessed it would come to this!

Now on to your most important question. The hulder-folk are a subset of the troll world. If you've read the pages from my father's journal that Granny Aino sent, you already know quite a bit about the hulder-maids. They are exceptionally beautiful, save that they have a cowlike tail and a hollow back. By instinct and training, they seek young humans to bring to their underground world. A youth who follows a hulder-maid this way will lead a prosperous life underground but lose his soul in the process.

More rare is the hulder-maid like Granny Aino, who will, for love, come to the human world.

On the other matter, you did indeed surprise me. In fact, I am flabbergasted that you have met Nettie Thump! My best guess is that your handshake with her somehow brought your huldra heritage rushing to the surface. If you had never met Nettie, you might have gone your whole life (which, by the way, will likely be quite a long one) without showing any signs of your huldra background beyond your gift for storytelling and your way with animals.

I am sorry not to have been a more attentive grandfather, Cody. I told myself that with your father so angry with me for returning to Finland when I did, it was better to stay in the distance. The move was a choice he could not understand and I could not explain. But I see now that hanging back was wrong.

Do not hesitate to contact me with any other questions that arise. And give my regards to Nettie Thump! Though I never met her, I have long been fascinated by her story. I never imagined she would end up in New York City!

Love,

Grampa Raimo

PS: Have you noticed anything strange about your farts?

Text messages between Cody Takala and Raimo Takala

Cody

How did you know about the fart thing?!

Raimo

Because I have the same problem. It's one of the side effects of being part huldra. Oddly, for some reason it doesn't happen to huldra themselves.

Cody

It's so embarrassing!

Raimo

I know. But not much you can do about it. How do yours come out?

Cody

They smell like roses!

Raimo

Interesting. I get lily of the valley.

Cody

How do you deal with it?

Raimo

Well, I haven't eaten beans for forty years. But basically you just get used to it. The condition skipped a generation with your dad.

Cody

Lucky him!

Raimo

Look at it this way, Cody. Odds are good that with your huldra blood you'll be tall, handsome, and rugged . . . with farts that smell very pretty. There are worse things to have as the family genetic markers! I can tell you from personal experience that as long as you can keep the farts quiet, so girls don't know where the smell is coming from, they will find the odors very attractive. You should have a very good love life.

Cody

GRAMPA!!

Raimo

You'll thank me later on. Trust me.

From: R.Takala@finnet.fn
To: C-Tak@kid2kid.com
Date: 10/20
Subject: About That Prince

Dear Cody,

Now that you know about me being half huldra, it might not surprise you to learn that I have access to a lot of information hidden from most humans. It's one of the reasons I chose my career as folklorist. I have even been inside Troll Mountain!

Because of this, I have a stock of things I haven't written up for publication. Sometimes this is because they are mere fragments of stories, unfinished and thus unsatisfactory for the average reader. Other times the information is just too sensitive to release to the human world.

Anyway, the point of all that is that after our last exchange of text messages I went digging through my files for something I had a vague memory of recording a couple of decades ago. It took me a while to find it, but it was worth the search. I am attaching it, as I am sure it will be of interest to you. It would probably also be of interest to Nettie, though she may find it disturbing.

I will leave it to you to decide whether to share it with her. Her story is already such a sad one that I would hate to make things worse for her.

Most people would think this is a mere fairy tale, of course. But now that you know about trolls and huldra and the Enchanted Realm, I'm sure you won't have any trouble believing it.

I can vouch for my source. He is a tonttu named Aspen Markonnis, and we have been friends for many years. He is highly placed in Troll Mountain, so I can promise that this is all true.

Now that I know Nettie is still alive, I plan to do some investigating to see what else I can find out about this. Though it has been many years, I may even go back to the mountain! (Wish me luck!)

Love,

Grampa R

PS: I am so happy to be in touch. I truly regret the long silence that separated us!

THE CURSE OF HEKTHEMA

From *The Annals of Troll Mountain*
By Aspen Markonnis

When Queen Hekthema failed in her plan to marry her daughter to Prince Gustav Fredrik, she was filled with both wrath and fear.

The wrath was due to her daughter's betrayal. By showing the prince her true face, Nettie had demolished a carefully laid plan.

The fear was at what Nettie's father (who was, after all, the King of Troll Mountain) might do when he learned of his wife's failure and his daughter's disobedience.

After two nights of brooding (as she told me herself, when I asked her what had happened), Hekthema hatched a new scheme. If they could not drag the prince under the mountain as their daughter's captive groom, they would have him in another way.

With that in mind, Hekthema disguised herself as a human crone, seemingly too old and withered to be a threat to anyone. Then she left Troll Mountain, carrying with her a basket of apples, one of which was specially enchanted.

It was this apple with which she planned to snare the prince.

The troll-hag stationed herself in the same place where her

daughter had met Gustav Fredrik on those occasions that led to his falling in love with the disguised girl. For three days and three nights she waited for the prince to come that way again. When he did finally appear, he was sullen and downcast, still mourning the loss of the beautiful maiden he had thought he loved until she revealed her true and trollish nature.

When the prince drew close, Hekthema stepped into the road and croaked, "Apples! I have apples, ripe and red. Will you buy one, sir?"

Despite being wrapped in bitter sorrow over his loss, the prince took pity on the crone. "I'll buy an apple of you, Mother," he said as he gave Hekthema a silver piece worth a hundred times the price of an apple.

She handed the prince the apple she had prepared

especially for him. Bright and shining on the surface, it hid poison in its firm and juicy flesh. With the first bite, Gustav Fredrik swooned and fell to the ground.

Hekthema dropped her glamour. At once her appearance shifted from a bent and withered woman to the powerful troll-hag she truly was. Throwing back her head, she uttered a growling cry. In response, seven tonttus burst from the forest and lifted the prince's senseless body. Swiftly and silently they bore him to the glass coffin Hekthema had prepared for his long sleep.

Then the tonttus carried Gustav Fredrik, coffin and all, into Troll Mountain.

From that day to this, the beautiful prince has slumbered in the glass coffin, guarded by the seven little men.

And none knows how to wake him.

Text messages between Cody Takala and Alex Carhart

Cody

Hey, Alex! You there?

Alex

Yep. What's up? Angus getting on your nerves?

Cody

No, he's fine. He keeps telling me what a pleasure it is to spend time with someone who is naturally tidy.

Alex

He would! Actually, the state of my room is starting to bug me. When are you bringing him back?

Cody

Not sure. It's not like you live only a few blocks away. I can't just say, "Hey, Mom, can I go over and visit Alex?" And I can't pop him in the mail. Besides, I think I'm going to need him for a while longer. Things here are getting weirder.

Alex

Weirder than you being able to talk to cats?

Cody

Yeah. Turns out I might be part troll.

Alex

Jeez, Cody, you've told me some whoppers, but that's pretty far out even for you.

Cody

It would be . . . if I was making it up! But I'm not. Seems that handshake I told you about brought some of my troll aspects—like being able to talk to cats—to the surface.

Alex

Not tracking here. Why would a handshake do that?

Cody

Because Ned Thump, the person I shook hands with, is actually a troll.

Alex

Get out of town!

Cody

It gets weirder. Turns out not only is Ned not human, he's not even a guy! SHE is really a troll named Nettie.

Alex

Why was she pretending to be a guy?

Cody

I think it was just easier for her. She's huge and really ugly. Now I need your female take on something.

Alex

Girl trouble?

Cody

NO! Well, sort of. It's about Nettie. I'm going to email you a couple of things I got from my grandfather in Finland. One is sort of a fairy tale, except it's totally true. The other is an unfinished story, but it's true, too. What I need to know is whether I should tell Nettie about the second thing.

Alex

This is nicely mysterious. When are you going to send?

Cody

Soon as we end this conversation.

Alex

Then let's end it. I'm dying of curiosity!

10/24

After I got Alex's text message I had a long talk with Angus about how to tell Nettie that Prince Gustav Fredrik is still alive, that he's imprisoned in a glass coffin, and that her mother is the one who did it.

His first response was that we shouldn't.

"Saints and marshmallows, boy!" he cried. "Do you know how messy that will be?"

"What do you mean?"

"Trust me, lad . . . when you get to mucking about with love, things always get messy. And you know I canna abide a mess!"

"But don't you think Nettie has a right to know?"

"What good would it do? To begin with, she's here and the prince is in Troll Mountain, on the other side of the Shadow Sea. Secondly, it's her own mother who's holding the prince prisoner. And thirdly, it's not as if Nettie could wake him."

"How do you know that?"

"Well, it has to be true love's kiss, doesn't it?"

"I don't know. The stuff Grampa Raimo sent said no one knows."

"Well, true love's kiss is the way that sort of thing usually works."

"Well, Nettie truly loved him. So if that's the way it usually works, she should be able to wake him."

"You're not paying attention! *She* loved *him*. But *he* did not love *her*. He fled from her! So what's the point in telling her?"

"I don't know. I just feel like we ought to do something."

Angus crossed his arms and scowled at me. "You know, 'twas my da getting mixed up in matters of love that brought about the curse that forced me to come to Alex."

"Well, that didn't work out so bad, did it? The two of you seem to like each other."

Waving his tiny fists in the air, he cried, "You great sentimental slop of a boy, have you heard a thing I've been saying?"

Then he stomped away, muttering to himself.

I was glad Alex had warned me about his temper. Taking a deep breath, I counted to ten to calm myself, then started on my homework.

An hour or so later Angus came stomping back—as much as someone who is only twelve inches tall can stomp—and said, "All right, we'll tell her! It's what my da would have done, so I suppose I should, too. But don't think I'm happy about it!"

So that's settled.

I hope I can talk Dad into letting me go back to the station with him again tonight. We have important news to deliver!

Tuesday, Oct. 25

I am in an agony of joy and confusion!

Cody sought me out again last night. I did not want to talk to him, felt I was not ready for that, so when I saw him coming I turned to hurry away.

"Nett—" he cried. "I mean Ned! Wait!"

Fortunately, there was no one nearby to hear him. But that he had almost shouted out my real name enraged me!

"Ned, it's important! I have something you need to know."

I turned in a fury and growled, "What is it?"

Cody looked frightened, so I probably sounded even harsher than I had intended. But I was still very upset about him discovering my secrets and wanted him to leave me alone. He took off his backpack, and I realized he had brought the brownie with him.

"I told the lad 'twas nae a good idea, and you would not want to see him," said Angus, sticking his head out of the pack. "Even so, I do think you'll want to know this."

"What is it?" I said, trying to restrain my anger.

"Um . . . can you read?" Cody asked.

"Of course I can read," I snapped, even though it wasn't an entirely unreasonable question now that he knew I was a troll.

Hand trembling, Cody held out a paper. "My grandfather lives in Finland. He studies folklore and collects stories. That was how I knew your story. . . . I read it in one of his books! But what people don't know is that one reason Grampa is so good at folklore is that he is half huldra and—"

"What?" I shouted.

He smiled. "My grandfather is half huldra. Which means I'm one-eighth huldra. Grampa thinks that's what caused that jolt when you and I shook hands. The skin-to-skin contact pulled my huldra part to the surface."

I looked at my hand in amazement.

"But that's not the important thing right now!" Cody continued. "The important thing is that Grampa has connections in the Enchanted Realm. When I told him I had met you, he was very excited and decided to do some new research. Yesterday he sent me this. I wasn't sure whether I should show it to you, so I asked my cousin Alex. She said I should definitely give you the information. So, um . . . here it is."

I took the papers he was holding and was startled to see my mother's name. But that was nothing to the astonishment I felt when I read the whole thing and discovered that Gustav Fredrik is alive and being held prisoner in a glass coffin! Joy at the news and fury at my mother's actions warred within me. My head began to swim. I think I may have actually staggered, because Cody cried, "Are you all right?"

"Yes! No! I don't know! Leave me alone! I need to think!"

I must have seemed very frightening, because he turned and ran.

I wanted to go back to my cave and curl into a ball. But I have made it a point of honor never to shirk my duties as watchman. So I faithfully followed my rounds until the night was over.

But my mind was focused entirely on what I had read.

Gustav Fredrik is alive . . . alive and imprisoned by my mother in a magical sleep!

What am I going to do? What *can* I do?

10/25

Someone must have pressed down really hard on the weirdness accelerator for my life, because this evening things moved into high gear.

It started when I got home from doing my jobs at Granny Aino's apartment. As I walked under the sycamore tree that stands near our building's front door, I heard a squawk. Looking up, I saw a large black bird perched on the lowest branch. It squawked again, as if calling to me, then turned its head from side to side. I had an eerie feeling it was checking to see if anyone was watching. That feeling was confirmed when it leaned forward and said softly, "You're Cody, right?"

Too shocked to speak, I just nodded.

"Good. I have a message for you."

A month ago I would have totally freaked out. But since then I've met a brownie, talked to a couple of cats, found out that I'm part huldra, and learned that my dad has a troll working for him.

So I only freaked a little.

"What's the message?" I asked.

"It's tied to my leg. Go up to your room and open the window so I can come in. I don't want to chance being spotted down here."

When I didn't move fast enough, the bird made an angry squawk and said, "Mice on a bun, boy, get going before someone hears us!"

I hurried into the building and up to our apartment. Once I was in my room I closed the door.

"Welcome home," said Angus, who was tidying my desk (even though it was already quite neat).

"Thank you," I said, heading across the room.

Just then the bird landed on the window ledge. As I grabbed the sill to raise the glass, Angus shrieked, "Moon and stars, Cody, what are you doing? You're not going to let that thing in, are you?"

"I am not a thing!" said the bird as I raised the window. "I am a raven, and a trained messenger. And fear not, small person. I have no interest in eating you. You would probably be sour and bitter."

Angus scowled, but I could see he wasn't sure how to answer. Claiming he would actually be sweet and tasty was obviously not the best response!

"Do you want to come in?" I asked the raven.

"Thank you," it replied, stepping over the sill. "I couldn't enter without being invited. I appreciate your asking, since I've had a long flight and could use a rest before I have to turn around and go back."

"Back to where?"

"Finland."

I stared at the raven. "You flew all the way from Finland? That's thousands of miles!"

The bird shrugged its ebony wings. "I came via the Enchanted Realm. The Shadow Sea that divides the continents in the Realm is not as wide as the ocean in the human world. And I'm a powerful flier. That's how I got my name."

"Which is?"

"Korkea Lentäjä. It means High Flier."

I tried to repeat the name. The bird laughed when I mangled it and said, "Call me Korkaya. If you don't mind, I'll spend the night here, then head for home in the morning. Now I'd appreciate it if you would take the message off my leg. The binding itches."

"Who is it from?"

"Your grandfather." The bird paused, then added, "He's in a bad situation."

"What's wrong?" I cried.

"It's all in the message. Take it out and read it."

I moved closer and saw a slender leather tube bound to the bird's leg. My fingers trembled as I undid the thin laces. When I was done, the bird flexed its talons and said, "Thank you. That's a relief!"

I pulled the message from the tube.

Dear Cody,

The reason I am using a raven instead of text or email to deliver this message is simple: I am being held prisoner inside Troll Mountain and electronics do not work down here. Fortunately, Korkaya is both strong and smart, and I have every hope that he will reach you.

The reason I am a prisoner is that I made a grave error in returning to the mountain: I underestimated how badly things have changed here, and how fierce a tyrant King Wergis has become.

I should, I guess, have been more discreet. I was not, and word of my questions about Gustav Fredrik got back to Wergis. From what I've been told, he had not thought much about the prince in recent years. Once reminded, he grew angry all over again that his daughter had revealed her true self and ruined their plan to capture the prince as her husband.

A troll can hold a grudge for a long time.

Fortunately, he does not know where the queen has stashed the glass coffin. And Hekthema is not willing to tell him because she is afraid that if he finds it, he will smash it. What makes that particularly bad is that if the coffin is not opened properly, the prince's sleep will end and he will die writhing in agony within the first hour.

I do have an ally here, my old friend Aspen Markonnis. And Erkki, the tonttu who brings my meals, is a friendly little fellow. He likes to gossip, and so loves the bits of old stories I can tell him. He has told me, in turn, that word in the mountain has it that Hekthema goes to gaze at the prince on a regular basis. The tonttus think she has fallen in love with him herself! But she has seen the King's anger and does not go now for fear of revealing where the prince is hidden. (In case it's not clear, Troll Mountain contains a vast maze of tunnels and passages.)

If the King does find the coffin, I fear it will be the end for the prince, and a nasty one at that.

I will say no more, in case this letter is captured before it reaches you. That is why I have not named your friend—you know the one I mean—who might have an interest in this information.

I suggest you read this letter to Askeladden. He may have some useful advice.

Love,
Grampa Raimo

10/25 (late)

So frustrating! Mom wouldn't let me go back to Granny Aino's, since I had already been there once and she didn't see any need for me to go back on a school night. Which means I can't read Grampa Raimo's letter to Askeladden until tomorrow.

And Dad didn't want me to go to the terminal with him tonight, so I can't talk to Nettie, either.

I think I'm going to burst!

Wednesday, Oct. 26

Last night I went to Mr. Takala and told him I was not feeling well and did not think I would be in tonight. I could tell he was startled. And why wouldn't he be? This is the first sick day I have taken in all the time he has known me.

But I was not lying, as some of my fellow guards occasionally do when they want a night off. I truly am sick at heart.

Yet I am also alight with happiness. The prince still lives!

It is a strange combination of feelings.

Anyway, I need some time to be alone, because I have more emotions than I know what to do with.

I wish that I could weep. I think it might help calm what feels like a volcano inside me.

I fear I may erupt instead.

Oct. 26

Dear Grampa,

Good grief! I can't believe you are a captive in Troll Mountain! I feel like I need to do something . . . but I can't figure out what!

I am sending this message back with Korkaya, who is leaving to return home in just a few minutes. I hope he has a safe flight.

This afternoon I will read your letter to Askeladden, as you suggest. And tonight I will seek out you-know-who to pass along your news.

Wish I could write more, but I have to go to school.

I don't think I will be able to concentrate!

Your grandson,

Cody

Wednesday, Oct. 26

I pace my cave, but I can find no peace, no hope, no solace.

The prince is trapped in a glass coffin. It is sealed by magic and he might stay there forever, neither dead nor alive, locked in an enchanted sleep created by my horrible mother.

I have no way to reach him, to save him, to help him.

Would he even want my help, he who fled from me? And if he did, how could I give it to him? I don't know how to wake him. I would need to learn that from Mother.

Mother.

Good grief, what would it be like to see her again? I have so much anger against her in my heart! Could I speak when I saw her, or would I only roar out my long-held fury?

And what of the prince? What would it mean to wake him? There are no more princes in Finland, after all. What could he do, what place find in this world, after his long sleep?

Would it be better to simply let him rest in peace?

And why do I even ask myself these questions, when I have no way to reach him?

10/26

This afternoon the weirdness accelerator moved into overdrive. I thought it would be best to have Angus with me when I read Grampa Raimo's letter to Askeladden, so I stopped at home to collect the little guy before I walked over to Granny Aino's apartment.

When we got there I made Askeladden swear he wouldn't chase the brownie. I was a little worried about him thinking Angus would make a good cat toy. Once I was satisfied Angus was safe, I let him out of my backpack.

After the introductions had been made, I did as Grampa Raimo had suggested and read his message to Askeladden.

The cat closed his eyes and listened intently. When I was done he said, "This is not good. Fortunately, I know what we need to do. I watched you snooping around the other day, Cody. Oh, don't deny it! I saw you, and you know it. So I know you're aware of the safe hidden in the wall behind the buffet."

"It's the weirdest safe I ever heard of!" I answered. "I have no idea how to get into it."

"I do," replied the cat with a grin and a stretch. "At least, I hope I do. It depends on how strong Aino's bloodline runs in you. Okay, the first thing you have to do is empty out the buffet so you can get at it."

Remembering my snooping, I said, "But there's nothing on that side but a solid piece of steel."

The cat laughed. "That's exactly what anyone poking around here is *supposed* to think. Now, empty out that buffet."

Grumbling to myself about bossy cats, I did as Askeladden ordered. Angus looked on with interest but had the courtesy not to comment.

When I finally had everything cleared away, the cat said, "Press your right hand flat against that red circle on the right side."

I did as he commanded. My hand covered most of the circle, but the few bits still visible began to glow. "It's getting warm," I said.

"Good. That means we have a chance! Now say this: 'By the huldra blood that flows within my veins, I, Cody Takala, order you to open to my touch.'"

I repeated his words exactly, then cried, *"Yow!"*

"Don't pull your hand away!" Askeladden ordered.

It was hard not to. The red circle had become so hot that it hurt. Gritting my teeth, I held my hand in place. Just when I thought I couldn't stand it any longer, the heat vanished. Better yet, with a small *click,* the door opened by a fraction of an inch.

I grabbed the edge of it with my fingernails, pulled it all the way open, then bent to look inside.

All I could see was blackness. It was as if a veil of perfect dark covered the safe's interior.

"Reach in with your right hand and pull out what you find," said Askeladden.

I stretched my hand forward. When my fingertips touched the veil of darkness, a jolt of energy tingled up my arm.

I yelped in alarm.

"Don't pull your hand back!" ordered Askeladden, his voice urgent.

It took everything I had to stay in place.

As I reached farther into the safe, the tingling grew stronger. It was weird, but not really painful. I kept reaching . . . and reaching! I had seen the safe from the other side, so I knew the cube was only a foot high, a foot wide, and a foot deep.

So why could I stick my arm in all the way up to my shoulder?

At last I felt something smooth and circular. I closed my fingers over its upper edge and pulled it toward me.

It came out of the safe with a *pop* and a *hiss*.

Once it was in the open I let go of it and began to massage my arm, which still tingled as if it had fallen asleep.

I stared at what I had retrieved. It was some kind of metal pot, about half the size of a volleyball. As I studied it, I realized it was like a tiny version of a witch's cauldron.

"Why is Granny Aino keeping *this* in a safe?" I asked.

"Gosh, I don't know," Askeladden replied. "Do you suppose it might be because it's valuable?"

Great. I now had two magical helpers—a brownie and a talking cat—and both were masters of sarcasm.

"Is there anything inside it?"

"Why don't you find out?" replied the cat, sounding amused.

I sighed and rolled my eyes, then reached into the miniature cauldron.

At the bottom I felt some folded-up papers.

I pulled them out.

The first sheet contained a set of instructions, carefully printed by hand.

The second, also handwritten, but in cursive, not printing, was from Granny Aino herself.

Instructions for Use

This cauldron is the property of the Takala family. Only someone of our bloodline can wake its power. To prove your right to use it, make a cut in the tip of your index finger, then rub it against the cauldron's rim.

If the cauldron accepts your blood as true, it will grow warm and hum a deep welcome. However, if the blood is rejected, the iron will grow cold. The finger will be frostbitten and possibly fall off.

So beware, ye of false blood, and tamper not with this cauldron!

Once woken to the trueblood's touch, the cauldron will be a trusty vehicle to carry you over land and sea. Simply grasp its rim and say, "Cauldron, I wish to travel!" At once it will begin to grow. It can expand to accommodate as many as six passengers.

When the cauldron has reached the size you desire, release the rim and it will stop growing.

Climb in and insert the key. When it begins to glow, name your destination, then spit three times over the edge.

The cauldron will rise.

If you are in the Enchanted Realm, it will begin to fly at once.

If you are in the human world, the cauldron will transport you to the Enchanted Realm before it carries you to the chosen location. If you seek a place in the Realm, the flight will end there. If your destination is in the human world, the cauldron will again cross the magical border when the flight is complete.

This cauldron is mine as Bride Gift.

This is true, though it was not actually given to me. I took it . . . as was my right!

Huldra tradition says the firstborn daughter is owed one treasure from the family stores, and this was the treasure I chose when I decided to marry Harald Takala.

By this cauldron my beloved and I escaped the wrath of my kin after we were wed. In its safe and warm embrace we flew to America, where we made our new home.

It is ours, and will pass to our descendants, now and forevermore.

—Aino Takala

10/26 (continued)

When I finished reading, my heart was pounding. Looking at Askeladden, I said, "Does this mean we could take Nettie home . . . not to mention try to rescue my grandfather?"

"Sounds like it to me," said the cat, swishing his bushy tail.

"We could, but it would be a terrible idea!" said Angus.

In my excitement, I hadn't really thought about what this meant. Angus was right. The idea of going to Troll Mountain was terrifying.

"Maybe my dad could do it?" I said.

"He'd likely lose his finger to frostbite if you could even get him to try waking the cauldron," said Askeladden. "He's never shown any sign of his huldra heritage. No, I'm afraid it will have to be you, bucko."

Partly to change the subject, I said, "Well, what's this about a key?"

"Oh, think, Cody!" the cat snapped.

I remembered the metal rod in the strongbox.

Part of me wanted to jump up and shout "YES!"

Part of me wanted to go curl up in a corner and pretend none of this was happening.

Only I couldn't do that. Because it wasn't only Nettie Thump who was needed at Troll Mountain. If I had the way to do it, and I did, I had to try to rescue my grandfather.

Then I realized another problem. "I can't just head off to the Enchanted Realm! My parents will be worried sick when I don't show up at home."

"No problem on that front, lad," said Angus. "Fearing it might come to this, I brought along my time peg."

"You have a time peg?" Askeladden said, sounding astonished.

At the same time, I said, "What the heck is a time peg?"

"'Tis a marvelous device," said Angus. "You'll remember I brought the peg with me when I volunteered to go home with you."

"Yes, but you were very mysterious about it."

"It is not to be spoken of lightly. I was given it by Granny Squannit, who is of the Enchanted Realm in this part of the world. She's an Old One, you know . . . so fiercely powerful it makes my toes curl even to think of her. The peg is why your cousin Alex and her brother and sister were able to travel to the Enchanted Realm with me to break the family curse."

"Alex and Bennett and Destiny have been to the Enchanted Realm and she never told me? I am so gonna clobber her for that!"

"No clobbering," said Angus solemnly. "She was

sworn to secrecy . . . as will you be, though I suppose you can tell her, since you both will have been there."

"So what, exactly, does this time peg do?"

"It locks us to a moment here in the human world while we travel in the Enchanted Realm. All we need do is pound the peg into the ground at the spot where we intend to enter the Realm. The peg will tie us to that instant, so when we return we will reenter the human world at the exact time that we left."

"As long as no one moves the peg," muttered Askeladden.

Which made me a little less enthusiastic about the situation.

Still, I couldn't wait to tell Nettie!

10/27 (evening)

At the worst of all possible times, Nettie has gone missing!

Dad told me she (well, actually, Dad still thinks Nettie is a HE) stayed home sick last night and sent a message that "he" would be out tonight as well.

It is desperately important that I tell Nettie there's a chance we can do something about the prince . . . especially since her father is *even now* looking for that glass coffin to shatter it!

It took me a while to figure out how to ask Dad where she lives without making him suspicious. Finally, I came up with the idea of saying I wanted to send a get-well card. Dad knows I've been talking to "Ned," so I guess that didn't seem too unusual. He said he didn't know the address offhand but would text it to me from his office.

It was a post office box! They send her paychecks to a P.O. box!

So where does she actually live?

I've been racking my brains, and I have come to a wild conclusion.

Nettie is a troll.

She is comfortable underground.

She told me she lives close to work.

It's a scary thought, but something inside tells me I'm right.

I'm at Granny Aino's right now. Supposedly I came over to watch a movie—a reward for having my homework done early and acing a tough math test. The real reason I came over is that I need to include Askeladden in any conversation about Nettie.

When I had finished explaining the current situation, Askeladden said, "So where do you think the she-troll is holed up?"

I took a deep breath, then said, "I believe she's been living right under Grand Central. There are all kinds of levels and tunnels and forgotten spaces down there. It would be perfect for a troll."

"Then we must go there and try to find her," said Angus.

"You don't understand," I said.

"I certainly do," huffed Angus. "The she-troll is missing. We need to give her information. Therefore, we must look for her."

"I mean you don't understand about Grand Central. You haven't been there, except in my backpack when we came back from Destiny's birthday party. The place is enormous . . . and the area underneath is even bigger. Some of the tunnels stretch out for miles. No one even seems to be sure how many underground levels there are! There's no way we could track Nettie down under there."

Askeladden stretched, then said, "Don't be so certain, Cody. Is there any place you can be confident she has been recently?"

"Sure. I talked to her several times in the last couple of weeks, so there are those spots. And I know some of the other areas she has to check when she makes her nightly rounds."

"Well, since you know that, we should be able to find her."

"And how exactly are you goin' to accomplish that?" Angus asked, putting his hands on his hips.

Askeladden did yet another of his elegant stretches, then said, "I can track troll-scent better than any bloodhound can track a human. If I can pick up her trail, I guarantee I can follow it—though it might involve a lot of back-and-forthing while we trace the route she takes on her guard duties."

"No!" I said. "There's a better way. Nettie has to punch out every night after work. So we can just go to the time clock. The last time she punched out will be the freshest trail." Then I realized another problem and said glumly, "But her scent will be mingled with the ones from all the other guards."

"No problem there. I can easily pick out troll-scent

from human spoor. And since it's a good guess she headed straight for her lair after she last punched out, the freshest trail is the one we'll follow."

I didn't like the word "lair." It had a sinister quality and made tracking Nettie seem more frightening than when Askeladden had first suggested it.

But she had to know about the danger the prince was in . . . not simply sleeping, but in peril of having the glass coffin smashed open, which would cause him to fall into true death, writhing in agony as he went.

It made me shiver just to think about it.

Then I realized another problem. "How will I get you into Grand Central, Askeladden? I can carry Angus in my backpack, but there's no way I could explain to Dad why I'm bringing a cat."

"No fears," said Askeladden. "Just get me out of the apartment and down to the streets. I'll travel on my own after that. I do know how to ride the subways, after all."

"You do?"

Askeladden looked at me in surprise. "Good grief, Cody. After all this you don't still think I'm a normal cat, do you? I've been with your great-grandmother since before your father was born."

"Wouldn't he have noticed how weird that is?" I asked. "I mean, no offense, but cats don't live that long."

"Troll-cats do. And your dad never paid enough

attention to me to get suspicious. As far as he knows, I've been 'replaced' twice. That's why I'm called Askeladden the Third. But it's really been me all along." He licked his paw, then added, "Your great-granny got me via the troll network."

"The troll network?" I said, totally confused now.

"Did it never occur to you that if both Nettie Thump and your great-grandmother could make it to America, other trolls might have done so, too? There is a small but thriving community of one-headed trolls here in New York City."

I tried to reply, but the idea of a whole community of trolls here in the city left me too boggled to speak.

Askeladden sighed. "As I was about to say, I have done a lot of errands for your great-grandmother over the years. The subways are part of how I get around."

"Won't someone report you, or try to capture you, or something?"

"Not likely. People enjoy seeing cats in the subway. They figure we're there for the rats. Also, I'm good at skulking. Most people won't notice me any more than they would notice a shadow. So I will meet you at your father's office, and—"

"You know where it is?" I interrupted.

"Of course. Your great-grandmother has sent me there more than once to check on him. Aino tends to be a bit of a worrier, to be honest. Now will you be quiet so I can finish?"

I nodded.

"All right. I will meet you at your father's office. You lead me to the watchmen's time clock and I'll take it from there."

So that's the plan.

I'm excited, and also scared. Really scared. I don't think Nettie would hurt me. But I don't know how deep under GCT she might be living, and I've heard Dad tell Mom there are people down there, too. And not necessarily nice ones.

But Nettie needs to know what's going on, and she needs to know it as soon as possible.

So if my guess about where her trail will lead is right, tomorrow night we will descend into the bowels of Grand Central Terminal.

Part of me wishes we could go right now. But it's too late tonight.

So tomorrow night it is.

I must be out of my mind.

10/28 (late)

This was the most terrifying night of my life.

Part of me wants to forget it. Another part thinks I need to write it all down while it's still fresh in my mind.

I think I had better. Maybe doing that will help calm me . . . or at least help me stop thinking about it.

I won't go into a lot of detail about the first part of the night. Let's just say I arranged things so I would head for Granny Aino's to feed Askeladden a little later than usual but come home in time to go to GCT with Dad.

I neglected to mention that when we left for the terminal I would have a brownie in my backpack, and that instead of doing homework I was planning to head for the terminal's lower levels in search of a troll.

I got to Gran's about five-thirty, said hello to Norman the Doorman, then took the elevator up to the penthouse level.

At six o'clock I came back down with a box containing Askeladden. (That cat is HEAVY!)

"Whatcha got there, Codester?" asked Norman as I came out of the elevator.

"Just some stuff Granny Aino wants me to take care

of," I answered . . . which I figured was pretty close to true.

A normal cat might have meowed, or yowled, or scratched at the box and messed things up. Fortunately, I didn't have to worry about any of that with Askeladden.

Once I was outside, I walked over to the ramp that leads to the building's underground parking area. I went down far enough to be out of sight of anyone on the sidewalk, then let Askeladden out.

"See you at the terminal," I said softly.

"See you there," he replied. Then he flicked his silver-gray tail and scooted up the ramp.

I hurried after him, but when I got to the sidewalk he had already disappeared.

I rushed back to our apartment, where I put a flashlight and a bottle of water into my backpack. Then I layered one of my T-shirts over all that to cushion it for Angus. "Hop in," I said, holding the sides of the pack apart.

He scowled and said, "You know, I do hate traveling this way. Ah, weel . . . I guess there's nothing for it." And with that he scrambled into the pack, made himself comfortable, then looked up at me and whispered, "All right, lad . . . let's go on a troll hunt!"

I hurried out of my room to meet Dad—I didn't want him getting cranky because I had made him late for work—and off we went.

An hour or so later, shortly after Dad left the office to check on his workers, Askeladden strolled in. I must have appeared relieved, because he said, "Don't look so shocked, Cody. I told you I would be here."

"I didn't mean to doubt you," I replied, blushing a little.

He flicked his tail and said, "Take me to the time clock."

I started out of the office. When I looked to see if the cat was following, I couldn't spot him! I glanced around and finally located him moving through shadows about ten feet away. He wasn't invisible, but you wouldn't notice him unless you were looking really hard.

He was definitely telling the truth when he talked about his skulking skills!

When I got to the clock, Askeladden came over to join me. I figured we were unlikely to be spotted, since at that point everyone had already punched in. He began sniffing around, muttering, "Troll trail . . . old. Troll trail . . . old. Troll trail . . . newer, but still stale." Finally, he said, "Ah, here we go! This is definitely the freshest of the lot. Follow me, Cody!" He trotted away, his tail straight up and waving like a silver ostrich plume.

As I had hoped, the scent didn't lead us through any high-traffic areas. However, after a while it did force us to cross some tracks. This was hard for me, since I've been told for as long as I can remember to NEVER do that. Askeladden had to coax me across.

Once we reached a place far enough from the main terminal that we were unlikely to be spotted, we stopped so I could let Angus out of the backpack. Grumbling about a cramp in his leg from the way he had been forced to travel, he positioned himself on my shoulder and took a grip on my collar. We resumed the hunt.

Now and again I could hear the scuttle of rats. Even worse was the moment when my flashlight beam fell on a cluster of them.

They were enormous!

Askeladden hissed and arched his back. Then he shook himself and said, "I would like to tangle with them. But we have more important things to do."

As I had both feared and expected, the trail brought us to a stairwell that led down to another level. Good thing I had Angus and a talking cat to keep me company. Otherwise I probably would have turned back. I'm fairly brave, I think . . . but not so brave I could have done this on my own. No way!

It was also good that I had brought my flashlight, because this level was not lit. On the other hand, I almost wished I couldn't see where we were, since it was downright creepy. And the smell . . . it was kind of like wet dog, but not anywhere near as nice. There were places where it reminded me of the streets up above when the garbagemen were on strike. Other places smelled strongly of pee.

In other words, it was nasty. As I swung the flashlight around, I saw some odd lumps against a far wall. When I realized that what I was seeing was blanket-covered people trying to sleep, I shuddered and quickly moved the beam away.

We had walked a little farther when I heard the *ploink ploink ploink* of dripping water. I swung the flashlight's beam in a half circle and saw dark pools that shimmered with an oily skin.

Beyond one of the pools rose a wall covered with a huge mural done by some graffiti artist . . . an angel with an arrow stuck in its chest, flying above a city street. The image was beautiful but also disturbing.

"Who paints a giant picture in a place that's always dark?" asked Angus. "And how did they do it?"

I had no answer.

We continued on, picking our way over discarded building material: chunks of wood, steel bars, concrete blocks, and so on. I tried to be careful but stumbled several times anyway.

The air was dank. Sometimes it reeked with sewage, or other nasty things that I couldn't name. I was amazed that the cat could continue to sense the trail.

I was starting to worry about getting back before Dad noticed I was missing when the cat led us into a tunnel that seemed to go on forever. Sometimes it was cool and dry. Other times we passed through odd spots of steamy warmth.

How far from the center of the terminal did Nettie live?

After a while the tunnel opened into an area so wide the beam of my flashlight couldn't reach the walls.

"We're still on the trail," said Askeladden. "Her scent is very strong here."

Seconds later an unfamiliar voice cried, "Who goes there?"

The words echoed from the walls around us.

"I said, 'Who goes there?'" repeated the voice angrily.

More echoes.

"Just some friends," called Angus, his own voice surprisingly strong. I hadn't realized the little guy could be so loud.

"What's your name?" asked the voice, closer now and definitely unfriendly.

"Angus!"

"We've no Angus living down here," snarled a different voice, louder, fiercer, closer.

"Run!" yowled Askeladden.

That definitely seemed like the best idea at the moment. Keeping the flashlight's beam on the ground directly ahead, terrified of tripping over some rock or piece of discarded track, I sprinted forward.

Angus, clinging to my collar, whispered, "If I fall off, lad, don't stop. I can take care of myself."

I didn't have time to wonder if that was true. I ran faster. At the same time, I found myself screaming, "Ned! Ned, are you here? I need you!" I was desperately hoping that I was right that she lived down here—and even more desperately hoping that she wasn't far away.

I peeked over my shoulder and saw a beam of light behind us. Whoever was chasing us also had a flashlight. That made sense but also meant he could move as fast as we did.

Looking behind was a serious mistake, because as I did, I stumbled and fell. My hand hit hard and the flashlight rolled out of my fingers. Even as I felt a new level of panic, I discovered something astonishing: I could still see!

Before I could think of what that meant, a third voice cried, "Get them!"

"Get them!" cried other voices, seemingly all around us now. "Get them!"

"Ned!" I shouted again. "Ned, are you here? NED!"

Our first pursuer was so close I could hear him panting behind me. Suddenly, a strong hand grabbed my arm.

I screamed.

At the same time, I felt Angus jump from my shoulder.

"What are you doing, kid?" growled my captor, giving

me a hard shake. "You don't belong down here! Wait . . . what?"

"Leave the boy be, ya great slobberin' dafty, or I'll tear your ear clean off!" cried Angus.

"Who? What? OWWWW!" howled the guy who had caught me.

But he let go of my arm.

It didn't make any difference.

The others had surrounded us.

Shouting and swearing, they reached for me.

A DISTURBING VISIT

Tonight, with no knock or warning, King Wergis barged into my cave.

This is never a good thing.

"We are uneasy, sage," growled his middle head. "We fear some disturbance coming our way. Tell us what it is!"

"I am not a sage," I replied, trying to hold down my panic.

The king's temper has always been unpredictable, but in recent years it seems his wrath is ever closer to the surface. "I am but a poor scrivener who sometimes sees the truth upon the winds," I said.

"And what truth do you see upon the winds this night?" his right head demanded. As usual, that head focused on me with its left eye only, the right eye simply rolling in useless circles.

The tusks of all three heads gleamed in the light of my candles.

I have made a sketch of the moment, as I have learned that doing this will sometimes save me from repeating the moment in my dreams.

"What did you see?" demanded his left head.

"That nothing lasts forever, and all are subject to change," I replied, cringing because I knew that though my words were true, he would hate them.

"LIAR!" roared all three mouths. "We shall be king for all our days!"

Yet I knew I had spoken the truth. Nothing lasts forever. Not even the reign of this ever more tyrannical king.

Friday, Oct. 28

I was pacing my cave, distraught and fretful, when I heard a distant scream, followed by a voice calling my name.

I was instantly alert. Was it Martha?

Another cry, and I recognized the voice.

Cody!

What in the world was *he* doing down here?

I scrambled out of my home and raced in the direction of the boy's screams. I can see fairly well in the dark, and it soon became clear that he was surrounded by a group of undergrounders.

They were angry. Even worse, though he was only a boy, they were frightened of him. This fear fed their anger . . . and fear-fueled anger is the worst of all kinds.

It took only a moment to realize why they were so disturbed. Cody had nothing of the underground about him—his clothes were clean and without holes; he was well fed; his skin was a healthy pink, not a pasty white. He was obviously not of our world, and if he was allowed to return upside and tell others what is down here, it would threaten all of us.

And that was a threat the undergrounders would not tolerate.

But picking on someone smaller than yourself is a thing *I* will not tolerate! With a ferocious roar, I hurtled forward. Seizing the first man I came to, I threw him aside.

I did the same with the second.

And the third.

At the same time, I heard the yowling of a cat. To my surprise, I also heard it hiss, "If you value your eyes, get your hands off me!"

A troll-cat?

Another voice, smaller, shouted, "Leave go, ya narsty brute, or I'll gnaw your finger straight to the bone!"

So Angus was also part of the fight.

I continued to thrash around me. Stray beams of light flashed over the battle. Some illuminated my face. When the undergrounders realized it was me, saw that I was fighting against them, they turned on me.

"Let this be, Ned!" shouted one. "You know we can't let him return now that he's seen us!"

"I know no such thing!" I roared as I thrashed about, flinging men in all directions.

Someone grabbed my shoulders. At once I flung myself backward, crushing him with my great weight. Ignoring his screams, I sprang to my feet. More and more of the men fell—some cursing, some screaming—as my fists connected over and over. Finally, the last of them fled whimpering into the darkness.

When all were gone, and all was quiet, I turned to

Cody. My voice low but ferocious, I growled, "Are you insane? What in the world are you doing down here?"

The boy cringed, then said the only thing that could have calmed my anger: "I came to bring you news about Prince Gustav Fredrik."

Which was how he became the first human I ever invited to my cave.

10/28 (continued)

"Cave" is hardly the right word for Nettie's underground home. The place is magical, and amazingly beautiful.

Hmmm. I wonder if that's my huldra blood speaking.

No, I think anyone would be delighted to enter this place.

To begin with, it's illuminated by stones of many colors. Some glow softly in muted tones. Others sparkle like giant jewels lit from within. With its rainbow mix of colored light, her cave reminded me of our living room at Christmas when only the tree is shining.

Well, it was somewhat brighter than that. Or maybe not. With my newly discovered dark-vision, it was hard to tell exactly how bright it was.

One thing I could see quite clearly was that Nettie's living room has a waterfall!

Seriously, a waterfall. It comes in over one high, rocky wall, tumbles down to a pool big enough to swim in, then runs across the floor and disappears through the far wall.

Nettie Thump, troll, has a waterfall, a pool, and a stream in her living room!

And it's pure, clear water, as I found later when Nettie offered me a drink.

If I had a room like this, I don't think I'd ever leave home!

However, the cave wasn't the only surprise. She had come running to my aid so fast she hadn't bothered to put on a hat. She had long hair that hung down past her shoulders!

"I'm sorry I don't have chairs," Nettie said. "But the only reason for chairs would be for visitors, and that is not something I ever planned on."

She paused, looked down at the cave floor, then raised her head again. Taking a deep breath, she said, "What is this news you bring me?"

I braced myself, then replied, "Prince Gustav Fredrik is alive, which you already know. That's the good news. The bad news, which I got from my grandfather yesterday, is that your father is seeking the prince's coffin and wants to smash it."

"But that is good, too," she said. "Then Gustav Fredrik will be free!"

"No, it's not good at all, Nettie! If the coffin isn't opened properly, if it's simply smashed, the prince will die an agonizing death."

Nettie clenched her fists and unleashed a wail of grief that seemed to travel down my spine. Fearing she was going to mistake messenger for message and whomp me senseless, I barreled on. "Listen! If you want to save the prince, I think I have a way to get us to Troll Mountain."

She fell to her knees so that she was looking directly into my face. Her enormous nose nearly touching mine, she said, "Tell me!"

So I did.

There's no turning back now.

Tomorrow night, if all goes well, we fly to Troll Mountain.

PACKING LIST

Flashlight
Extra batteries
Snacks
Bottled water
Warm clothes
Boots
Cell phone (will it work in the Enchanted Realm?!?)
Cat food
Knife
Time peg
Hammer (for time peg)
Key to the cauldron!!

Dang! This won't all fit in my backpack. I think I'm going to need my duffel bag instead.

10/29

It's 10 p.m. on Saturday and I am in Granny Aino's apartment, where I'm supposedly watching movies on her giant TV. Mom is out on a major gig. Dad has tickets to a big game. Grampa has his weekly poker night. So they were glad to let me come over here, and happy to use Norman the Doorman as a hands-off babysitter. (Norman doesn't check on me, but he's always there in case of emergency.)

Angus and Askeladden are with me. Angus is pacing and muttering, which I understand. Askeladden is sleeping as if nothing amazing is about to happen.

I think only a cat could do that.

Once Nettie gets here, we'll start the evening's real business . . . our journey to Troll Mountain! But she isn't due until midnight, and I'm not sure how I'm going to get through the next couple of hours without exploding.

That's actually why I'm writing this. . . . I have to have something to do to distract myself or I'll go nuts!

What if this doesn't work? It seems insane that the cauldron can fly us to the Enchanted Realm. Of course, what's even scarier than the question "What if the cauldron doesn't work?" is the question "What if it DOES?"

If it does, I have to go. I mean, I can't leave my grandfather a prisoner in Troll Mountain if I have a way to try to rescue him!

But what is the place going to be like?!?

Okay, calm down, Cody. Let's discuss the plan.

It starts with a trip to Central Park. This is because we discussed all kinds of places to pound the time peg into the earth and that was the eventual choice.

I don't particularly like it, but nothing else seemed to work.

My first suggestion was that we pound the thing into the soil around one of Granny Aino's potted plants.

"I'm nae sure that would work, lad," Angus said. "I suspect the peg needs to be driven into the world itself. More real that way."

"I suppose you're right," I said.

"Even if he's not, this isn't something we want to take a chance on," said Askeladden. "So I'm with the brownie. Drive it into real ground."

"Okay, what about the garden behind the apartment?" I suggested. "That's close by, and safe."

"Safe from outsiders, yes," said Askeladden. "But you know how fussy Marvin is. If he spots a peg in his precious petunias he's likely to pluck it out and toss it in the trash."

Marvin is the building's gardener, and Askeladden was right. He would *not* put up with a stray peg in his domain!

If he found it, which was likely, who knew what time we might end up returning to the human world?

"What about one of the trees outside the building?" I suggested.

Thousands of trees line the streets of New York City, mostly growing from square plots of earth surrounded by sidewalk. But here we faced the same problem: someone might pull the peg out because it didn't belong. With hundreds of people passing by most trees every day, we couldn't chance it.

"You wouldn't think pounding a peg into the ground and having it stay there would be such a problem!" I said in frustration.

Finally, we decided on Central Park. The place is enormous—seriously, it's so big it's got seven lakes and ponds!—and there are plenty of wooded spots where people would be unlikely to notice the peg.

I know I said before that New York City is safe if you don't go to the wrong place at the wrong time. But there's no way in the world I would go to Central Park on my own late at night. Thankfully, I won't be alone. I will have Nettie Thump with me. I can't think of anyone safer to be with. No one in his right mind would attack someone as huge as she is!

Wait. My phone just buzzed.

It's Nettie.

OMG. It's happening!

Nettie, written *afterward* . . . date in human world uncertain

Going into the upper world is always difficult. Though the people of New York City accept a lot, I know I will be stared at, even if that staring is done on the sly.

I know I will be talked about, even if it is only once I am out of earshot.

I know I will be laughed at, even if it is hidden by the polite hand, or the turned-away face.

In the hope of attracting somewhat less attention, I changed out of my uniform and put on a "street outfit." Still male, of course. It's fairly hard to find clothes that fit me, though once I found the Big and Tall Shop this got easier. But I cannot imagine trying to buy a dress in my size.

I assembled a small bundle of things I would need, then made my way up to the terminal, being careful to avoid the other guards, which I could do because I know their routines. Then I used the subway (I have to duck to get on the train) to get to the neighborhood where I would meet Cody.

People are very good at averting their eyes on the subway. It's a New York specialty. But when I reached the right stop and went to the streets of "up above," I heard the usual gasps, noticed the usual staring. Still, nobody bothered me. And nobody laughed out loud, which I appreciated.

I had to walk seven blocks to reach the building where Cody's great-grandmother lives. Once I was there and staring up at it, I considered turning and heading back to my cave. But even though the idea of seeing my mother again filled me with anxiety (and the thought of possibly seeing my father filled me with terror), there was no turning back. Gustav Fredrik needed me, and I could never live with myself if I let my courage fail me now.

I did feel bad about dragging Cody into this. But he and the brownie had made it clear that the cauldron would not work without him. Besides, I knew Cody planned on trying to rescue his grandfather even if I didn't join the expedition. Being aware of that, I felt I owed it to Cody's father, who has been so good to me, to accompany the boy.

And, to confess the complete truth, I had begun to be fond of the sprat, annoying as he could be. The thought of him venturing into Troll Mountain on his own was not something I could accept.

Not knowing, then, what an astonishing part he would have to play in the events to come, I took out my cell phone and called his number.

10/30

It's been a long time, and almost no time, since I have written here. That's because it was just last night that I wrote the last entry. But so much (soooo much!) has happened since then.

Our journey to Troll Mountain is the first thing I need to write about, because . . . well, because it's where things start. Also because it was amazing.

When Nettie called my cell to tell me she had arrived, I told her I would be right out. I put on my winter coat— totally wrong for the weather in New York City, but we were heading for a mountain in Finland!—and hoisted my duffel bag. (Angus had climbed into it when he heard me talking to Nettie.) With Askeladden trotting at my side, I left the apartment and headed for the service elevator. There was no way I could get past Norman the Doorman at this time of night, so we had to go out the back way.

I met Nettie at the corner and we headed for the park. I suspect we looked like a homeless guy and his kid out to find a place to sleep for the night.

It was seventeen blocks to the spot where we had decided to enter the park, which is officially open until 1 a.m. (We got there about twelve-thirty.) We went straight to a cluster of trees I had scouted out earlier and made our way to the center of it.

When we felt we were well hidden from prying eyes, I took the cauldron out of my duffel bag. The moon was only a quarter full, but with my newly discovered night vision I could see pretty well. As Nettie, Angus, and Askeladden looked on, I took out the knife I had packed and cut my finger.

Man, that was hard. I flinched and pulled back the first three times I tried. When I finally *did* manage to make the cut, it hurt like holy heckenlooper!

I rubbed my bloody fingertip against the cauldron's rim, hoping it would grow warm, terrified that it would become cold and all this would have been for nothing. . . . Not to mention I might get frostbite, or even have my finger fall off!

The cauldron did not grow warm, but it didn't get cold, either.

It just sat there.

"It's a fake!" I said angrily.

Nettie moaned in despair.

"Don't give up yet," advised Askeladden. "You are three generations down. It might be that the cauldron is confused, trying to decide whether to accept you."

I rubbed my finger over the rim again. Doing that hurt, because of the cut.

Nothing happened.

"Try again," said Askeladden. "They say third time's the charm . . . and sometimes it really is."

Not really comforted by that "sometimes," I did as the cat suggested and rubbed my finger over the rim one more time. As I did, I felt a burst of warmth.

A deep hum rose from inside the cauldron.

"It's working!" I whispered.

The others cheered—but very quietly.

Following the directions, which I had read so many times I knew them by heart, I grasped the rim and said, "Cauldron, I wish to travel."

It began to grow! It was slow at first, but the bigger it got the faster it expanded.

"Stand next to it, Nettie!" I said. "Tell me when you think it will hold you comfortably."

It wasn't until the cauldron was almost up to my shoulders—which made it only waist-high on Nettie— that she said, "Enough."

I let go of the rim.

Instantly the cauldron stopped growing.

"I'll get in first," said Nettie. "You stay out so you can pound in the time peg."

I nodded and pulled the peg and the hammer out of my pack.

Once Nettie had climbed in, I lifted first Angus and

then Askeladden to her so she could lower them into the cauldron.

That done, I pounded the time peg into the ground beside a tree I had chosen (and carefully memorized!) earlier.

"I hope you work," I muttered to it.

Back at the cauldron, I wondered how I was going to get in. I had put my hands on the rim and started to haul myself up when Nettie said, "Let me lift you."

I was a little annoyed. I mean, I'm kind of old to be picked up. On the other hand, next to Nettie I was like a little kid, so I said, "I guess you might as well."

She plucked me off the ground, lifted me over the rim, then looked down into the cauldron and said, "Watch out, here he comes!"

Once I was in place, Angus tugged on my pant leg and said, "Put me on your shoulder."

I reached down to get him, thinking that now I knew how he felt.

"I want to watch, too," said Askeladden. "Pick me up, Nettie."

"Actually, I think it would be better if I crouched down," she replied. That made sense. There was plenty of room for her now, and it seemed perilous to fly with so much of her above the cauldron's rim. What if she fell out?

"Ready," she said.

"Me too," said Askeladden, who had climbed to her shoulder.

"The time has come, lad," said Angus. "Put in the key!"

I pulled the metal rod from my pocket and inserted it into the hole in the rim. It began to glow, exactly as the directions had promised! Grasping the rim on either side of the key, I said, "Cauldron, take us to Troll Mountain!"

Then I spit over the edge three times.

A moment passed.

Another.

Then the cauldron trembled and lifted slowly into the air.

I knew that was what was supposed to happen. Even so, I gasped in astonishment as the cauldron rose above the trees. Suddenly we shot forward. A flash of light nearly blinded me. At the same time, a weird tingle swept across my body.

"You did it, lad!" cried Angus. "We're in the Enchanted Realm!"

Still seeing spots from that flash of light, I looked over the edge of the cauldron. The city had vanished. Below us stretched a mix of forest and open land, with some occasional cottages. In only moments we had passed over that and were flying above water.

I looked up. The sky was clear, velvety black and

spattered with the brightest stars I have ever seen. I don't know if that's because we were in the Enchanted Realm, or simply because we were away from the "light pollution" of the city. The moon was full—it hadn't been in the human world—and seemed enormous.

I had expected it to be colder, but the cauldron kept us warm.

I had no way of knowing how fast we were traveling. It's not like the cauldron had a speedometer. Even if it had, I didn't have any idea how far we had to go. Korkaya had said, and Angus had confirmed, that the Shadow Sea is smaller than the human world's Atlantic Ocean. But how much smaller, neither of them seemed to know.

I took out my cell phone, wondering if it could tell me what time it was in the Enchanted Realm.

The screen was blank, as I had pretty much expected. I slipped it back into my pocket. Then for a long time I stood clutching the rim of the cauldron and gazing ahead, around, and down.

At one point I was pretty sure I saw a sea serpent.

A few minutes after that, Angus tugged my ear and said, "Look over there!"

I turned and gasped when I spotted a trio of dragons winging their way across the sky. Their bodies showed dark red as they passed in front of the moon. I would have loved to see them up close but was also relieved that they didn't appear to notice us.

We flew on.

Sometime later we saw three ships. Their sails glowed silver in the moonlight.

"Elves," whispered Angus.

Then for a long time there was nothing but water.

Lots and lots of water.

It was late and I was tired, with no idea of how much longer the trip would take. Since I wasn't steering and had nothing to do now that the cauldron was locked on our route, eventually I slid down until I was resting against its side. I wanted to stay awake but knew I should sleep. I needed to be ready for whatever happened when we landed.

Askeladden crawled into my lap. "You did a good job getting us started, Cody," he said softly.

Given how sarcastic the cat could be, this made me happy.

I had a snack, then drifted off to sleep, thinking about the fact that I was flying through the Enchanted Realm in a magical cauldron, accompanied by a talking cat, a Scottish brownie, and a troll.

✦ ✦ ✦

I don't know how long I'd been asleep when Askeladden nipped my ear and said, "Better wake up. Nettie says we're close."

I yawned and stretched, then realized Angus was sleeping against my side. Looking up, I saw it was now daytime. Nettie was standing, her hands gripping the cauldron's rim as she stared straight ahead. She had put on sunglasses and a big floppy hat that shaded her face.

I hauled myself to my feet and gazed out.

The Shadow Sea was gone. Below us now were snow-topped mountains, thick with pine trees on their lower slopes.

The cauldron began to slow.

"It's hard to tell which of these is Troll Mountain," fretted Nettie. "I've never seen it from above."

"That's all right," I said. "The cauldron will know."

"Yes, I trust that," she said in her deep voice. "But where will we touch down? Troll Mountain is big, and it will be cold once we leave the cauldron. We don't want to land in a place where we will have to walk for hours to find an entrance. And we want to avoid most entrances, anyway, since they may be in use." She paused, then said, "I do know of a secret entrance that would be good if we can find it."

"Does it have a name?" I asked. "Maybe the cauldron can take us to it."

"It's called the King's Door. It would be a safe place to enter . . . as long as my father is not using it right now."

I nodded, grasped the cauldron's rim, and said, "Take us to the King's Door!"

The cauldron made a right turn, circled halfway around the mountain, then slid gracefully down onto a wide ledge that opened onto a cave.

I swallowed.

Hard.

It was time to enter Troll Mountain.

Nettie, afterward (continued)

Cody removed the key from the cauldron. Instantly the cauldron began to shrink, crowding us together.

"Put the key back!" I whispered urgently. "PUT IT BACK BEFORE IT CUTS US IN HALF!"

He tried to do so but dropped it!

"I'll get it!" cried Angus, leaping from Cody's shoulder to the ground. He tossed the key back up, and Cody managed to catch it. But by the time he jammed it back into the cauldron, the thing had grown so small we were nearly trapped. Askeladden, caught in the bottom of the cauldron and standing on top of my feet, was yowling bitter complaints.

With some effort, Cody managed to wriggle himself out. Once he had done so, I was able to step out, too. As soon as I was out of the way, Askeladden leaped up to the edge.

"Do not ever, *ever* do that to me again!" he hissed furiously.

"Sorry," said Cody. "I'm still learning!"

He leaned into the cauldron to get his duffel. After he retrieved it, he removed the key again. In only moments the cauldron shrank to its normal size. Cody picked it up and put it into the bag.

Then we all looked at the entrance to the mountain.

"What's that smell?" asked Cody, making a face.

"Home," I said, feeling an unexpected burst of happiness.

"No offense," Cody replied, "but it smells like rotten eggs."

"Yes, that comes from the lava."

"Lava?" Cody yelped.

I looked at him in surprise. "Didn't I tell you? Troll Mountain is a volcano."

WHY IT IS NICELY WARM IN TROLL MOUNTAIN

From *A Troddler's Guide to Life*

Our comfort here in Troll Mountain is largely due to the wisdom of our elders, who long ago took steps to care for us all. The reason we are snug and warm in our caves and caverns and tunnels is simple: Troll Mountain was once a volcano, and at the heart of the mountain there is still a bubbling pit of lava.

Wise are the elders who saw how this could help us. With the aid of our cousins the tonttus (who, being small, were more suited for this), we dug passageways that carry the heat of the lava to all the corners of Troll Mountain.

Tonight when you go to sleep in your stony troll bed, remember to thank the elders, without whom your sleep would be cold and uncomfortable!

Sleep well, little troddler, sleep well.

(Author unknown)

Nettie, afterward (continued)

"We're going into a volcano?" cried Cody, staring at the entryway in horror.

"You don't need to worry," I told him. "The lava is way down at the bottom of the mountain. It's what keeps us warm."

"Oh, I see," he muttered. "Sure. Makes perfect sense."

But he didn't move.

"Shall we go in?" Angus asked, after another minute or so.

"Not yet," I whispered. Cody wasn't the only one who was hesitant. I was confused by the mix of emotions cascading through me. This was home, the home I had left more than a hundred and fifty years earlier.

The home where I had been treated so badly, but home nonetheless.

Inside the mountain were my mother, who had been so cruel to me, and my father, who had been crueler still.

And yet they were still my mother and my father.

Why did I care what they thought of me, what they would think when and if they saw me?

Why, being terrified of them, did I at the same time long to see them?

And what of the prince I had come to rescue? Could I do it?

And if I did, what would it mean? Would he simply flee from me once more?

Why not? I am a troll, after all, and he is human. But somehow he had my heart, even after all those years. He was beautiful, that is true. But it was not his beauty that had caught and held me. It was his kindness, the only true kindness I had ever known at that time in my life.

I realized that was why I would do anything to rescue him. His kindness had left its mark on me.

10/30 (continued)

It was cold on that ledge, and I was starting to shiver. I wanted to get inside the mountain where it was supposed to be warm. (Smelly, but warm.) But I was also afraid of entering that tunnel, which would mean we were officially in the world of the trolls.

As I stared at the dark opening, a bird shrieked overhead.

A moment later Korkaya landed on my shoulder.

"I've been wondering if you would show up!" the raven said. "I'm glad I spotted you before you went in! Exactly how were you planning to find your grandfather, Cody?"

"Um . . . by searching?"

The bird whapped me with his wing. "Pigeons on toast, boy! Do you have any idea how long that would take? You could wander those tunnels for years looking for that hidden prison. I will lead you there."

"How do you know your way around?" I asked.

"I was raised inside the mountain, just like all the messenger ravens."

That was a relief. But it also made me realize something I'd been trying not to think about, which was that Nettie and I had different missions and would probably have to separate to carry them out. Having an enormous troll at my side had given me a sense of safety that I was soon going to lose.

I turned toward Nettie. She was sitting on a nearby boulder, pulling off her boots. Before I could speak, she said, "We will be parting soon, Cody. You must seek your grandfather, who has done me a great service by alerting me to the danger to the prince. I must go . . ." She stopped and swallowed hard, then said, "I must go to face my mother."

It was hard to imagine Nettie Thump being afraid of anyone. But knowing how my own mother can be when I cross her, I totally understood. I don't mean that Mom ever whacks me or anything.

It's that thing she does with the Mom Look.

I could hardly imagine what a Mom Look would be like when it was delivered by a troll . . . especially one as fierce as Hekthema!

Nettie, afterward (continued)

When we entered the mountain, I was surprised to find a tonttu standing guard.

"Who goes there?" the small person demanded.

"I am Nettie Thump, daughter of Queen Hekthema, returned from long exile," I replied. "Who are you, and why are you on watch here?"

The tonttu looked at me in amazement, then dropped to one knee and cried, "It IS you! Welcome home, Princess Nettie!"

This startled me beyond measure. "Am I truly welcome?" I asked. Then I added, "Also, please rise."

The tonttu stood and said, "I cannot speak for your mother or your father, but I can say for the tonttus that you are most welcome indeed. Things have grown dire here in the mountain. Your father becomes more harsh with every passing year. There is great discontent, not only among us tonttus but among the greater trolls as well. We have longed for you to return, for you were always good to us."

These words both stoked my fear and warmed my heart. Though I was glad the tonttus remembered me so fondly, I felt greater concern than ever about my defiance in returning. Living among humans, I had learned that their anger usually faded in time. But my father was no human. Had his wrath at my misdeed actually increased over the years?

"What can you tell me of Prince Gustav Fredrik?" I asked.

A look of terror crossed the tonttu's face. "Please do not speak of him. I would be risking my life to answer!"

I knelt before him and whispered, "If you have remembrance of any good I may have done you or your kin, please tell me."

Trembling, the tonttu said, "The glass coffin is hidden deep away—I know not where. The king seeks it daily, and daily when it is not found, his wrath increases. Your mother knows but will not tell, and the king dares not enrage her, for she is as fierce as he is."

This shocked me. Mother was never as strong as Father when I knew her.

"If you would find the prince, first find your mother," said the tonttu.

I resisted the urge to throttle him. It would have done no good and ruined my reputation among the little people.

"Will you let us pass?" I asked.

"Will the cat vouch for the human?"

"Certainly," said Askeladden. "Otherwise I would not bring him to your mountain. He is part troll. You can test him, if you want."

"No, no," said the tonttu. "If a cat such as you claims

he is all right, I will not question you. And the *very* small person, what is he?"

"I am a brownie, as you ought to know," said Angus. "You don't get out much, do you?"

The tonttu scowled, but I quickly said, "Angus is clearly of the Enchanted Realm and cannot be denied entrance. Now please stand aside."

"No," said the tonttu, surprising me. "Not yet." He went to the wall, where he took a gray cloak from an iron peg pounded into the stone. "The boy should take this," he said. "The cat and the raven will raise no suspicions, and the brownie is clearly of the Realm. But you cannot simply have a human boy walking around the mountain, even if he is, as the cat claims, part troll."

He handed the cloak to Cody. "We tonttus use these when we do not want to be seen by passing trolls. Huddle on the floor and pull this over yourself, and you will seem as no more than a boulder to anyone passing by."

Both Cody and I thanked the tonttu profusely.

"It is the least I can do to aid you on your path, Princess Nettie," he replied.

Then he stood aside and we walked past him into the darkness.

As we did, I began to sing.

10/30 (continued)

Even though I speak Finnish, I had no idea what the words to Nettie's song were. All I knew was that after a few seconds the walls ahead of us began to glow. Well, not the walls themselves. As in her cave under Grand Central, what glowed were certain stones embedded in the walls and ceiling. As they woke to her voice, they began to shine in a variety of colors. We soon went from complete darkness to a clearly lit path into the mountain.

As Nettie continued to sing, I realized that the light only extended about ten feet ahead of us. I looked behind and saw that once we had passed an area, it went dark again. It was as if we were traveling in a capsule of light that moved as we did.

We came to a place where the tunnel forked, and Nettie stopped. As the stones dimmed around us, she pointed to the right and said, "I must go this way."

"But Cody's grandfather is held in this direction," said Korkaya. He was sitting on my left shoulder and extended his wing to indicate the left fork.

"Then it is time for us to separate," Nettie replied, and I was touched by the sorrow I heard in her voice. "I will go on alone from this point. I must trust Angus, Askeladden, and Korkaya to serve you as faithful guardians, Cody."

"You can count on that, lass," said Angus, who was, as usual, riding on my right shoulder . . . which kind of balanced having Korkaya on my left.

To my surprise, Nettie next said, "I have a gift for you, Cody." She fished from her pocket a stone about the size of a softball. "I brought this from my home under Grand Central to light your way. Simply sing,

My friend Nettie bids you wake,
And light my travel for her sake

and it will glow for you. You will not get as much light as when I sing the tunnels into life, but it should be enough to travel by, especially now that your night vision is so improved." She paused, then added, "I know you brought a flashlight, but I think it better to use this. It will attract less attention."

I felt a lump in my throat. "Thank you," I murmured, accepting the stone.

Nettie put her enormous hands on my shoulders and said, "Cody, I do not know what will happen next, either with your quest or with mine. But I do know that you have made it possible for me to follow my heart and try to make things right after all that has gone wrong. I thank you for this, and give you good wishes for finding your grandfather. If you do, then use the cauldron to take him to safety."

"But how will we know what happens to you?" I asked.

"It is possible you will never know. You should leave the mountain as soon as possible."

"But don't you want us to use the cauldron to take you home?"

She drew a heavy breath, then said, "I no longer know what I want."

With that she stood, began to sing, and headed down the right-hand path.

I watched her go until the walls grew dim around us and Korkaya said, "Shall we continue?"

Lifting the stone Nettie had given me, I chanted the proper words.

Soon the stone began to glow.

With Angus on one shoulder, Korkaya on the other, and Askeladden walking before me, I entered the dark tunnel I hoped would lead to my grandfather.

THE PROPHECY OF THE MOUNTAIN'S HEART

From *A Brief History of Troll Mountain*

More years ago than memory can count, our troll-tribe claimed this mountain and made it our own. As the Age of Man crept on, driving the Enchanted into ever greater retreat, Troll Mountain remained our refuge and our haven.

But how long it will last, we cannot say.

The reason for this uncertainty is that carved into a tunnel wall near the heart of the mountain, where a gap in the rock lets us look down upon the liquid stone that bubbles and pops as it warms our underground world, is a most disturbing poem.

For one thing, it lacks the required fart of proper troll poetry.

But that is a minor issue compared to the prediction of a time when doom might come upon us.

No one knows where this verse came from, who wrote it, or who carved it. Some think it is a joke. But though many have tried, not even our greatest stone carvers have been able to add a single letter, or gouge one away. The prophecy remains untouchable.

Some believe that the great wizard Väinämöinen carved

it, after he had guided us here both to provide us safe haven and to separate us from the humans.

I do not know if that is true.

Mostly we try to continue with our lives, and not think about the prophecy too much.

But that has become more difficult in recent years. . . .

By Aspen Markonnis, Tonttu
Scribe of Troll Mountain

Prophecy of the Mountain's Heart

Deep *in the* **heart** *of our* **world** *is pure* **fire,**
Source *of our* **warmth** *and all* **that** *we de-***sire.**

Long *as it* **lasts** *will our* **world** *be se-***cure,**
King *must stay* **true** *for our* **world** *to en-***dure.**

If *king grows* **false** *and the* **stone** *starts to* **rise,**
Un-*derground* **home** *will soon* **face** *its de-***mise.**

Hark, *all ye* **trolls!** *Let not* **king** *crush your* **breath.**
If *that day* **comes,** *then your* **warmth** *brings your* **death!**

Sweet *be the* **scent** *that will* **warn** *doom is* **near,**
Rose *on the* **rise** *is the* **smell** *you should* **fear!**

—Author unknown

Nettie, afterward (continued)

I knew the way to my mother's cave, of course. It was where I had been raised, when I was not in the troddler nursery.

It was not a place of happy memories, and I was filled with dread at the thought of seeing Mother after all these years. Could I face her without crumbling? She had held such power over me once. But that was long ago. And now I had my rage to help me . . . rage at what she had done to me, and to Gustav Fredrik.

Yet there was also the fact that if she had simply left him alone, not caught him in this enchanted sleep, Gustav Fredrik would be long dead already, gone to dust as happens so soon with humans.

As I traveled, I passed tonttus scurrying about on errands. Some looked at me oddly because of the modern clothing I wore, but then diverted their gaze and hurried on. They seemed fearful and defeated, not like the lively creatures I had known when I lived here before. I had a dreary sense that in this behavior I was seeing the heavy hand of my father.

Trolls were also making their way through the tunnels, of course. I moved fast when I saw them, acting as if I was on important business . . . as, indeed, I was. But I would also avert my face, not wanting to be recognized.

I wondered if that was really necessary. How many would still know me after all this time? The tonttu guard had, but only after I had identified myself. No one was expecting me to show up here.

Because Mother and Father make their homes close to the heart of the mountain, more than once my path took me past the openings in the tunnel walls that look down into the bubbling lava pit that is our underground sun, source of our warmth and survival. As always, it was red as the reddest rose. And, as always, its odor was harsh and acrid. Yet it was the odor of home, and so struck something deep within me.

Then, finally, I was standing outside my mother's cave. It was large and magnificent, as suited the consort of the king.

I took a deep breath, and then another.

And then another.

Gathering all my courage, which felt tiny compared to what I was about to face, I stepped into the cave and said, "Mother, I need to speak to you!"

Those of us observing the troll world continue to be fascinated (and puzzled) by the changes we see occurring there.

Old trollishness, with all its ferocity and anger, is still quite clearly present, of course. But there seems to be a new strand of behavior rising, especially among the troll-hags.

I suppose this should not be a total surprise. It was noted long ago that the trolls began to change in response to the changes in the human world. As the human world continues to change, should we not expect the same of trolldom?

The great mystery, actually, is how closely are the two worlds connected . . . and, even more important, WHY are they connected?

What do these changes, most especially the rise of kindness among the younger generation, mean for trolldom overall?

Will there be some sort of crisis if this goes on?

Is it even possible that trolls might begin to interact with the human world?

The idea is staggering.

10/30 (continued)

With the stone for light and Korkaya continuing to provide directions, we made our way deeper into the mountain. I say deeper, because with few exceptions every tunnel we followed sloped gently downward.

The rotten-egg smell grew stronger as we descended.

"'Tis a fair stink indeed," muttered Angus into my ear. "I doubt any amount of scrubbing could get it out of the walls!"

Though there was a fair amount of traffic in the tunnels, we were usually able to draw aside into some niche—there were a lot of them—when we knew someone was approaching. We always had plenty of warning; even before the tunnel ahead would begin to glow, we could hear the singing of the tonttu or troll (the troll voices were much deeper, of course) who was bringing the stones to light.

More often than not, the traveler was a tonttu intent on some business, and not seeming to care that we were such an odd group—cat, raven, human boy, and brownie.

The trolls, however, were truly frightening. If we could not quickly find a niche or side tunnel, I would drop to the floor and pull the tonttu's cloak around me, hiding

Angus and the glow stone. The trolls were enormous . . . the largest of them could easily have gripped my entire head in one of his massive hands and then crushed it.

"Don't worry," Askeladden reassured me after the first incident. "Most of them are not very observant. And the more heads they have, the less they notice."

I saw that other groups sometimes had a cat, always of unusual size, walking ahead of them.

"Askeladden, is there something special about cats here?" I asked during a stretch of travel when no one was around.

"If you mean, are we recognized in this world for our full worth and value, then I would say yes, that is the case," he replied smugly.

After a while the air grew cooler and didn't stink so strongly. When I mentioned this, Korkaya said, "That's because we're moving away from the heart of the mountain now, toward the outer edge."

A final turn brought us into a passage that, after about a hundred yards, came to a dead end in a circular space. In the center of the opposite wall was a windowless wooden door, a single huge slab held in place by roughly worked metal hinges.

"This is the place," Korkaya said.

"Are you sure 'tis the lad's grandfather on the far side of that door, and nae some hideous monster?" Angus asked.

"Fairly sure," replied the bird. "It can be easy to get turned around in these tunnels."

Which didn't do much to make me feel more secure. But since it seemed as if there was no choice, I said, "How do we open the door?"

"You might try using the key," said Askeladden.

I sighed. "You know, the light is pretty low here, cat. And you can see better in the dark than I can. So have you spotted the key, or are you just being sarcastic?"

"Look on the wall behind you," said the cat, who was sitting with his tail wrapped around his front feet.

I turned. Sure enough, hanging from a metal peg that had been pounded directly into the cave wall was a metal ring. From it dangled two old-fashioned keys, one nearly a foot long, the other only about a third that size.

"It's over there so the prisoner can't reach it," said Korkaya. "Though that seems unnecessary, since there's no window in the door anyway."

I had to stretch up to lift the key ring off the peg. I crossed to the door. My hands were trembling, partly because I feared that someone would catch us trying to free the prisoner, partly because I was finally going to meet my grandfather, who had been so mysterious to me for so long.

The keyhole was at eye level for me, and it was clear that it required the bigger key. I inserted it, but my trembling fingers made it rattle in the lock.

"Hurry, Cody!" hissed Askeladden.

Finally I managed to work the lock. I heard a satisfying *click* and the door swung open.

I stepped into the cell.

On the far side was a stone table. Above it a barred window opened onto the outside world.

The man sitting at the table had turned toward us. He had broad shoulders and shaggy blond hair. One eye was covered with a black patch. But what made me gasp was that, aside from the patch, he looked so much like my father that for a moment I almost thought Dad had somehow ended up here in Troll Mountain.

Except he actually looked younger than Dad.

"Cody?" he cried, leaping to his feet. The action created a clanking sound, which was when I realized he was held to the table by a long chain. "You are Cody, right? What in the world are you doing here?"

"I came to rescue you. What did you expect after you sent that message and asked me to read it to Askeladden?"

"I expected you to provide Nettie with the cauldron so that if she truly wanted to, she could try to rescue the prince. I certainly didn't expect you to come with her!"

"But I *had* to come! The cauldron only works for someone in our family."

He blinked in surprise. "I didn't know that! Mother only told me the family *had* a magic cauldron. She never told me the rules for using it! I am so sorry, Cody. I didn't mean to drag you into this danger."

"Do you know how upset I would have been if I'd had to send Nettie off in that cauldron and hadn't been able to come myself?" I demanded.

My grandfather stared at me for a moment, then began to laugh. Not a scornful laugh, more a sound of delight. "I suppose I should have expected no less from my grandson." His face turned sober. "Even so, I am sorry you have done this. A crisis is growing in Troll Mountain, and it is not a safe place to be."

I glared at him, then put my hands on my hips and said, "I come all the way across the Shadow Sea to rescue you and that's all the greeting I get?"

His face twisted in surprise. Then he smiled and spread his arms. His voice low but filled with something deep and wonderful, he said, "Come here, Grandson! I am happier than I can say to meet you at long last! It has distressed me not to be a bigger part of your life."

"Why weren't you?" I asked, trying not to let too much pain sound in my voice.

"Look at me," he said. "Do I look like I could be your father's father? When he was growing up, it was fun to remain so youthful. But after a while it became strange, and upsetting. Though I was thirty years older than him, we looked nearly identical. When my wife passed away,

I decided it was a good time to move to Finland, where I was able to 'reset the clock' on how old I actually am. Your dad never quite forgave me for leaving. It has been killing me not to be more a part of your life."

That was all it took. I ran to his arms. He threw them around me, lifted me off the floor, and spun me in a circle.

Something deep inside me—the huldra part?—knew him, and knew at once that we were kin and we were close.

Finally, he put me down.

"Let me unlock your leg chain," I said, holding up the smaller of the two keys.

When I was done he said, "Thank you, Grandson. Now let's figure out what we should do next."

"Tell you what, boss," put in Korkaya, fluttering over to land on his shoulder. "First thing, why don't you close that door so it's not so obvious you're on the loose? Then say hello to the rest of us. *Then* we can talk about what to do next."

My grandfather nodded. "Correct, as usual, Korkaya."

He strode across the cell, extracted the key, and closed the door. "Don't worry," he said when he saw the look on my face. "It doesn't lock automatically. And we've got the key inside with us, thanks to you. Now, who is your other friend?"

When I introduced Angus, my grandfather said, "Clearly you've been up to even more than I realized,

Cody. You'll have to tell me about it in detail if we ever manage to get out of here."

"Getting out shouldn't be so hard. I've come with the family cauldron, so I can fly you back to the human world, wherever you want to go. But I feel like first we should make sure Nettie is all right."

He frowned. "Do you know where she is now?"

"She went to look for her mother," said Angus.

Grampa Raimo bent his head forward and ran his fingers through his hair. "I hope this doesn't blow up in our faces," he muttered.

"Why?" I asked. "What's going on? You said there was a crisis of some kind."

"It's King Wergis. He was always fierce, but he has grown much worse in recent years. These days even the largest of the trolls walk in fear of his wrath. There is no telling when he will lash out, what will upset him, what punishment he might decree. Rebellion is brewing, and the last thing we want is to be caught in the middle of a troll civil war. I hope Nettie will be able to free the prince, but if the king finds out she's here, it could be catastrophic. His anger at her has grown volcanic. I'm torn, Cody. We should leave as soon as possible. But I don't want to abandon Nettie if she needs our help."

I started to answer. Before I could speak, the cell door swung open and we heard a shout of alarm.

Nettie, afterward (continued)

My mother turned to me. I knew at once that I had spent too much time in the human world, for her face seemed even more hideous than I had remembered.

What had my exile done to my trollishness?

Her eyes grew wide when she saw me. For a moment I thought I spotted a fierce joy. But that look passed at once to anger, then confusion, then fear.

Afraid of me? That couldn't be possible. Afraid *for* me, for what my father would do if he found I had returned? That seemed unlikely as well. So my own confusion was complete.

Finally, she said, "Nettie, what are you doing here? Does your father know you've come back?"

I was surprised to hear what seemed like real concern in her voice.

"I have returned because I learned that Gustav Fredrik is alive and in danger," I said. "I have returned because I learned what you did to him." I took a deep breath, then added, "And I have returned because there is unfinished business between us."

My heart was leaping within me like the lava in the heart of the mountain. Though my hands were trembling, I managed to keep my voice steady. In tones of steel, I said,

"I need to know, Mother, how you could have done what you did to me."

My mother lowered her head in shame, something I had never seen before, never even imagined possible. Her voice soft, she said, "Your father made me do it, Nettie. I was weak. I should have protected you better."

This startled me almost beyond belief. I had never in any way imagined her to be weak.

Then I thought about my father, the most terrifying being I had ever met. And in that moment I understood that my mother, for all the strength I thought she possessed, might indeed have been living in fear of him.

I had to harden my heart against this, or the pain of that admission would have knocked me to my knees.

So I turned to the next question.

"How is my father? Of what temper? What mood?"

My mother's face twisted and she said, "His mood grows worse, daughter. Much worse. He is caught in a constant fury and has become a tyrant. All in Troll Mountain walk in fear of his anger, and that fear is made much greater because there is no telling what might trigger it, what might unleash the next wave of his wrath."

This chilled my heart, and I hoped dearly I could leave the mountain without having to see him.

I pressed on to the most important question. Hardly able to get out the words, I asked, "And what of the prince?"

"Gustav Fredrik is hidden deep away. Even so, he is in constant danger, for your father seeks him daily."

Her face was marked with a grief I had never thought to see there. She took a step forward and reached toward me.

I flinched.

"Nettie," she whispered. "Oh, Nettie, I have been mourning your absence for over a century. I have never forgiven myself for the part I played in your leaving."

Against my wishes, I felt a pang of concern for her and asked, "Are you all right?"

She shook her head. "I do not know. These are strange days. I am changing. We are all changing, all except your father. He clings to the past, clings to pride, clings to what he feels he is losing. The world outside our mountain moves too fast for him, and he is baffled in how to deal with it. Rather than finding a way to live with change, he digs in his heels and demands that it stop. But it will not stop, and the fact of that drives him to ever greater fury."

"I am sorry for that," I said, and truly meant it. "But he is no longer my concern. Tell me, is there any way to wake the prince?"

My mother's face grew bleak, and her next words caused me to stagger. "None that I know of."

After so much hope, after such a seemingly impossible journey, to learn that it was all for naught pierced me to the core.

"Then it is best to leave things as they are?" I asked.

Mother shook her head in misery. "No, it is not. Every day the chance that your father will find the coffin and smash it grows greater."

"And the prince will die if he does," I said. "But if we cannot wake him, he is as good as dead anyway."

My mother shook her head again. "It is worse than that. If the coffin is simply smashed, rather than being opened with the proper spells, the prince's body will indeed die. However, his unleashed spirit will wander aimlessly for all eternity. Now he merely sleeps. But if he is not released to death with gentle words and good intent, his spirit will roam the halls of Troll Mountain in endless misery and loneliness."

I stared at her in horror. "Then why have you not released him already?"

"I do not have the strength," she murmured, and for the second time I heard shame in her voice. Looking up at me, she wrung her hands and said softly, "We are not supposed to appreciate human beauty, Nettie, but he is the most beautiful thing in my life, and I have not been able to let that go."

"So you have held him at the cost of his soul," I said, nearly choking on my fury. Then, though each word seemed to scorch my throat as I uttered it, I snarled, "If you cannot do it, I will do it for you."

It was in that moment that I truly understood I must

indeed love the prince. If not for love, how else could I do this terrible deed?

"Better you than your father," replied my mother.

"Better me than my father," I agreed. "Now, take me to the prince."

Even as I realized it was not a request but a command, Mother drew a deep breath, nodded slowly, and said, "Follow me."

10/30 (continued)

Standing at the door of the cell was a tonttu. The little man carried a tray that held a mug and a couple of bowls. His expression kept changing, so it was hard to tell whether he was frightened, angry, or betrayed.

I suppose it's possible to feel all those things at once.

"Who are these . . . these *others*?" he cried. "Where have they come from?"

"Come in and calm down, Erkki," said my grandfather. "We have things you need to know."

Wide-eyed, the tonttu stepped into the cell. Still holding the tray, he kicked the door shut behind him. "Have I not treated you with respect and kindness?" he said bitterly. "Is this how you repay me?"

"Be sensible, Erkki," said Grampa Raimo. "With that door unlocked, I could have been long gone by now if I had wanted to. It's not as if I have fled from your care."

"Well, that's true," sniffed the tonttu as he set down the tray. Then he tilted his head and said, "Why *didn't* you flee?"

"Because we have important work to tend to and I need your help."

"You do?" said the tonttu. I could hear a hint of eagerness in his voice.

"We do," said Grampa R. "Let me bring you up to date. To start with, this is my grandson, Cody. Korkaya Raven you already know. The very small person is a brownie named Angus. He hails from Scotland, where his folk are not unlike the tonttu in how they relate to the human world. As for the cat, he belongs to my mother and—"

"I most certainly do not belong to your mother!" interrupted Askeladden. "I do not *belong* to anyone. I am . . . connected . . . to your mother."

"I stand corrected that you are connected," replied Grampa Raimo, smiling and bowing his head. Again he turned back to the tonttu. "The cat is my mother's companion. These three have come here for a purpose, and with news that will surprise you."

At the mention of news, the tonttu's eyes lit up and he said, "Do tell. You know I love a good bit of gossip!"

My grandfather smiled. Clearly he knew he had the tonttu. Voice low (even though there was no one but us to hear), he said, "Princess Nettie has returned to Troll Mountain!"

Erkki gasped and put a hand to his chest. "This could be wonderful," he whispered. "Or it could be the end of everything."

"Precisely," replied my grandfather. "Now, can you gather some others and help us? I am fairly certain that if she can get her mother to cooperate, Nettie will be heading for the prince. I would like to meet her there in case we can assist in whatever she decides to do."

The tonttu was fairly quivering with excitement. "I do not know the way, but I think I can find some who do. I will be back soon."

He dashed out of the cell, slamming the door behind him.

"What do we do now?" I asked.

"We wait. I have been cultivating Erkki as an ally since I was captured. He's a good-hearted little fellow but lives in terror of the king . . . as does everyone in the mountain these days. I've been lucky that Wergis has been too obsessed with finding the prince to pay much attention to me. Otherwise I might be in much worse shape than you find me in now. Well, never mind that. Let's see what Erkki left for us to eat."

"I'm nae sure the lad should partake of this food," said Angus.

"You're wise to be cautious," replied my grandfather. "And if we were in a faerie mountain, I would certainly agree. But he can eat this without fear of being trapped." He smiled and said, "He may not like it, but he can eat it."

"I'm starving!" I said.

Which seemed to settle the matter.

The tonttu had brought a fish soup, which reminded me of something Granny Aino makes sometimes. There was also a kind of bread, fairly hard but all right if you dunked it in the soup to soften it. The third thing was a mashed vegetable, bright orange.

"Troll root," said my grandfather, pointing to it. "It only grows on this mountain."

I had some of everything, as did Angus, though his portions were tiny.

Askeladden stuck with the fish soup. He said it was very good.

As we were finishing up, the door swung open once more. Erkki stepped in, followed by six more tonttus. Five were dressed in simple clothing. The sixth looked much more elegant, his dark tunic embroidered with gold symbols.

I noticed an odd look pass between him and my grandfather. But it was Erkki who spoke. "These five"— here he indicated the humbly dressed tonttus—"carry food to the tonttus who guard the glass coffin. They have agreed to lead you to the prince. I brought Aspen because he is the scribe of Troll Mountain and should be witness to this."

I remembered that Grampa Raimo was friends with a tonttu named Aspen. Clearly they were not letting on that they knew each other.

"You must pretend to be our captives," continued Erkki. "Otherwise we may be stopped along the way. The cat and the bird will be able to travel freely, as all ravens and cats do in the mountain." He paused, looked at Angus, and said, "The human boy I can explain, but it would likely be best if we could hide the brownie."

Angus sighed. "I can ride in Cody's duffel bag. I'm used to such indignities."

Erkki nodded and said, "Good." Turning back to my grandfather, he added, "I will need to bind your hands behind your back. The boy's, too."

"And we will need to trust you," Grampa replied.

"Of course," said Erkki as he bound my hands. "Now listen. The prince is hidden deep in the heart of the mountain. Only the lowliest of the tonttus, who must take food to the seven who guard the coffin, know the way. That is because the queen knew the king would not think to question them. . . . They are not important enough."

"Which tells you how pompous and out of touch he has become," said another of the tonttus. Then he waved his hand and said, "Whew! Something smells like roses."

"Sorry," I said. "I farted."

"Are you all right?" asked my grandfather. He looked worried.

"Not sure. Maybe I shouldn't have eaten that food. My stomach is kind of jumping around."

"We don't have time to worry about that," said Erkki anxiously. "Follow me."

He led us out of the cell, then closed the door behind us, carefully locked it, and hung the keys back in place.

"So as not to arouse suspicion," he explained.

With our tonttu escort singing the walls to a dim light, we reentered the tunnels and began to make our way toward the heart of the mountain.

I followed Mother down, ever down, toward the mountain's heart. As we traveled closer to the lava, the air grew warmer, the smell ever more pungent.

I could tell we were traveling by minor tunnels because the walls gave very little light compared to the more important routes. So I was surprised when I heard someone approaching from a side tunnel.

"Say nothing!" ordered Mother. "I will handle whoever it is."

I nodded and waited.

When the approaching group came into sight, I was astonished to see a band of tonttus escorting Cody and a tall human with blond hair in our direction. Most of the tonttus were fairly shabby, but one was quite well dressed and looked strangely familiar. He caught my eye and gave his head the tiniest of shakes, as if to warn me to say nothing. It was an old signal of ours, and I held in a gasp as I realized it was my companion in mischief from so long, long ago.

I assumed the tall human must be Cody's grandfather, though he looked far too young for the part. Both he and Cody had their hands bound behind their backs, which made me worried and angry. Korkaya and Askeladden were with them. I wondered where the brownie was, then figured he was probably concealed in Cody's pack.

"What is this, Grekko?" said my mother, her voice low but sharp. "Why have you brought these humans here?"

One of the tonttus bowed and said, "They told us what Princess Nettie hopes to do. We brought them to you in case their help was needed."

Quickly, I explained to my mother who Cody and Raimo were. Then I turned to the tonttus and asked, "If you brought them to help, why have you bound them?"

The tonttu leading the group said, "Because to let them walk as if free would have aroused suspicion."

I realized at once that he was right.

We walked on. After several minutes, the tunnel came to a dead end. I was afraid we had taken a wrong turn until Mother placed her hand against the wall and murmured some words I could not make out. With very little sound the wall parted, revealing that the tunnel actually continued into the mountain.

We passed through. Once we were all in, Mother spoke a sharp word. The wall slid shut behind us.

"That false wall is why your father has not discovered where the prince is hidden," she said. "It was the last protection. It would open to his touch, of course, for he is the king. But it is so well made he cannot see it."

"Would you please remove our bonds now?" asked Cody's grandfather.

The tonttus hurried to do as he requested.

We continued on, the downward slope steeper now, Mother always singing the walls to light ahead of us. The heat was becoming hard to bear, even for me. Soon Cody took off his jacket and set it against the tunnel wall. "I'll pick it up on the way back," he said.

"Carry it!" ordered my mother. "Even now I do not want to leave anything like a trail or a clue."

Cody picked up his jacket.

Shortly after that we turned a corner, and I gave a little cry, part excitement, part grief.

We had entered a cave that was a nearly perfect hemisphere. Directly across from us was a circular opening about three feet above the floor. Through it I could see the rosy glow of the lava. I wondered how far below us the mountain's heart might be. It was clear from the heat that we were close.

In the cave, just as the legend had said, were seven tonttus. Because of the heat they were almost naked, wearing nothing more than loincloths. Each held a spear or had one lying next to him. Though they were supposed to be on guard, some were sitting, some lying down. Three were playing some kind of game with knucklebones they rolled like dice. I gathered they had gotten used to not being disturbed by anyone except my mother. Even so, they leaped to their feet when we came in. Bowing in unison, they said, "Welcome, Queen Hekthema!"

Then they goggled at the rest of us, clearly wild with curiosity but uncertain whether they dared ask.

I thought little of all this. My attention was riveted to the center of the cave, where, on an altar of stone, rested the glass coffin that held Prince Gustav Fredrik.

His finely sculptured features, his high cheekbones and cleft chin, looked little changed since I had last seen him, a hundred and fifty years before.

I felt a tightness in my chest. We were here to set him free. But could I possibly bring myself to do that? It would be hard. Yet I knew I could not allow my father to shatter the coffin and thus doom the prince to wander in eternal despair as one of the unquiet dead.

"What do we do now?" I said to my mother.

"The cover is sealed in place. We need to sing it off. I could do it on my own, but it will be faster if we work together. Once the seal is broken, we will lift the lid from the coffin. After that it will take about an hour before he truly departs, his spirit safe to go . . . wherever it was supposed to go. We must guard him well until that happens!"

With a heavy heart I took my place at the foot of the coffin.

Mother stood at the head.

"Echo me," she ordered. Then she began to sing, her voice as harsh as I remembered it from those terrifying lullabies long ago. She would sing a line, and I would repeat it, not understanding the words, which were in a magic language she had never had a chance to teach me.

The others watched in silence, the only sound beside our voices the dull roar of the lava somewhere below. When we completed the second verse, I heard a slight popping sound. Mother nodded to me. We grasped the lid of the coffin and lifted.

It came off with no resistance.

My heart was pulsing with sorrow.

We placed the lid against the wall. Then I returned to the coffin and bent over it to gaze on the sleeping prince.

"We need only keep him safe for another hour. Then his spirit will be free," said Mother.

I did not answer. I was staring down at the prince.

Because I was standing with my back to the entrance of the cave, I did not see my father enter. I only heard his fearsome roar, and the heart-stopping words, "Faithless daughter! How dare you return to our mountain?"

I was so startled that I jumped, unintentionally pushing the coffin away from me. It tottered on the edge of the altar, then slipped over, carrying the prince with it.

I heard the crash of glass as it shattered on the stone floor.

A cry of grief I had not known it was possible for me to make tore from my heart.

Quivering with rage, I turned to face my father.

10/30 (continued)

As if my stomach wasn't already in enough of an uproar, Nettie's father storming into the cave sent it into overdrive. Seeing the king in all his fury was the most terrifying moment of my life . . . worse, even, than when I was attacked by the undergrounders while searching for Nettie below Grand Central.

About the king: to begin with, he had three heads!

He stood at least eight feet tall but seemed even taller because each head was topped by an iron crown that rose in wicked points. He was dressed in leather breeches, and a pair of wide leather straps made an X across his broad, hairy chest. From his shoulders hung a cape sewn together from the pelts of many animals.

Five of his bulging eyes, which were the size of softballs, literally blazed, almost as if there were candles inside them! The sixth eye, dull and dim, rolled in its socket.

Ferocious tusks thrust up from each of the three lower jaws. His shoulders hunched up behind him like a small cliff.

He had bristling hair and spiky, untrimmed beards.

I thought everything was over then and we were all

going to die. But to my astonishment, Nettie said firmly and without fear, "Father, you have no place here!"

The king bellowed . . . not a word, just an ear-shattering cry of rage from all three mouths.

Nettie's mother came to stand beside her. "Our daughter is right, Wergis. This is no place for you." With a scowl, she added, "And how did you find your way here?"

"Not all are disloyal to us," said the king's central head. It was smirking, which is an odd facial expression when you have tusks. "Erkki came to let us know that we might follow a group here to find the sleeping prince at last."

"Oh, Erkki," sighed my grandfather. I could tell he was terribly disappointed in the little tonttu.

"Well, you have done your worst," said Hekthema. "The coffin is shattered, as you can see. You have achieved your goal. Now go and leave us in peace while we finish what must be done."

The king's five good eyes burned with new fury. "You dare speak to us with such insolence?" he bellowed. "You dare defy our wishes, our orders, our commands?"

I noticed that the tonttu Aspen—my grandfather's friend—had moved to the window and was looking down at the lava. Suddenly he turned back. His face marked with fear, he cried, "King Wergis! The Heart of the Mountain is restless. I fear it is starting to rise!"

A silence fell over the cave. Aspen looked back through the opening, then turned. His voice thick with panic, he said, "It is! It is rising!"

This put a stop to everything. Was the mountain going to erupt?

The thought was horrifying. We would be drowned in lava!

And then it happened.

Angus had been right—I shouldn't have eaten the troll food. Not because it would magically trap me here in Troll Mountain. Just because it didn't agree with me.

Without intending to, I unleashed the biggest, most powerful fart of my life. It was silent but potent and seemed to go on and on and on. The sweet odor of roses filled the cave, overwhelming even the rotten-egg smell of the lava.

"Roses!" cried Aspen, his voice filled with horror.

"Roses!" cried the other tonttus, their faces twisting in fear. "Roses! Rose on the rise! The end is coming! The end is coming!"

"Your Majesty," said Aspen, "as your sage and advisor, I tell you that if you would save the mountain, you must go now, and go quickly! You know the prophecy:

Sweet be the scent that will say doom is near,
Rose on the rise is the smell you should fear!"

"Rose on the rise," chanted the other tonttus. "Rose on the rise! The smell we should fear."

Wringing his hands, Aspen said, "The prophecy is coming true! If you do not leave quickly, all of Troll Mountain will be destroyed!"

All three heads of the king looked horror-stricken.

"Smell it, Your Majesty!" urged the tonttu. "Whenever did roses cover the smell of the lava? You have vowed always to protect the mountain. It is your oath! You cannot stay. *You cannot stay!*"

The king growled as his three heads sniffed the air. The rage that twisted his features made me fear he might simply pick us up one by one and toss us through that window, down into the rising lava.

Instead, he roared in helpless fury. Then the central head bellowed, "Troll Mountain will stand! Never will it fall because of King Wergis!"

He turned and strode toward the tunnel that led out of the cave. At the entrance, he spun back and said to the tonttu who had urged him to go, "Let it be noted in the Annals, Aspen Markonnis, that when the time came King Wergis sacrificed all to save Troll Mountain."

He reached up and one by one yanked off those fierce-looking iron crowns and flung them to the cave floor. Each bounced several times before coming to rest. He glared around the cave with his five blazing eyes, then turned and disappeared into the darkness.

For a long time, no one said anything. Finally, my grandfather went to the tunnel. He stared into it, then turned to us and burst into laughter.

"Oh, that was well played, Aspen," he said when he could catch his breath. "Tell me, was the lava really rising?"

"It was indeed," replied the tonttu. But as he said it, he winked at my grandfather. So I couldn't tell for sure whether he meant it.

Grampa Raimo turned to me, bowed, and said, "Grandson, I must congratulate you on what may be the greatest and most well-timed fart in all of history! With that ripe and rosy scent you drove a tyrant from his throne!"

The air of jubilation that filled the cave was interrupted by a wail from Nettie.

I turned but couldn't see her until she rose from behind the stone altar.

Her face was twisted in grief.

From her massive arms dangled the limp body of the prince.

Nettie, afterward (continued)

The moment my father was gone, I hurried behind the stone altar. The sparkling shards of glass that littered the floor did not bother my bare feet. Overwhelmed by sorrow and tenderness, I knelt and gathered the prince in my arms.

Then I returned his body to the altar.

Mother and I had failed, failed miserably, in our attempt to protect him until his spirit could be properly released.

Now that sweet soul would be damned to wander for all eternity.

Looking down on his handsome face, knowing it was the last time I would ever see it, I could not resist. Expecting nothing, but secretly hoping true love's kiss might yet do its work, I bent and pressed my lips to his.

He did not stir, which did not surprise me.

I heard a choked sound from my mother. I turned and saw that she was wringing her hands in despair.

I returned my gaze to the prince. As I did, I felt something surge within me, a wave of emotion as fiery and powerful as lava rising in a mountain shaft. I placed my hands on the edge of the altar to support myself. Whatever was happening to me continued. A wave of pain and despair that surpassed all the suffering I had experienced to this point boiled in my heart.

Then I realized it was more than mere despair. The feelings running through me included an overwhelming tenderness for this man who had shown me the first and only tenderness I had ever known . . . and had paid for it by being cast into this false death, which would lead to his everlasting torment.

It made no difference that the kindness he had shown me had come while I was under a glamour, displaying a false beauty. Until Gustav Fredrik, I had never known what kindness was, or what the heart could experience. Though he had woken something in me that might better have been left slumbering, it could never go to sleep again.

I saw it, now, in how I had treated little Martha. My small kindnesses to her came from what I had learned from the prince.

As I gazed down on him, remembering all that, my eyes began to sting.

I lurched back in shock.

Was I about to weep?

No, that was impossible!

"TROLLS DO NOT WEEP!" I shouted.

But the next instant, a sob burst from my chest . . . a sob pulled from a place so deep inside me that I had not known it existed. At the same time, warm droplets flooded my eyes and rolled onto my cheeks.

I was horrified, terrified, knowing that to weep is utterly untrollish. Yet I could do nothing to stop it. The tears poured down my cheeks to fall upon the prince's face, upon his full lips, his high cheeks, and most of all on his eyelids, those eyelids so long closed in magical sleep.

Eyelids that now, impossible as it seemed, flickered open.

I backed away, expecting the prince to scream or cry out at the sight of my hideousness.

Instead, Gustav Fredrik smiled, lifted his hand to my cheek, and whispered, "There you are! I've been looking for you for such a long time." He gazed around, then said, in total confusion, "But where am I? I was sure I was out searching for you. Was it all a dream?" He shook his head. "How long have I been dreaming? Where am I? How did I get here?"

"My mother ensorcelled you," I said, feeling embarrassed. "You have been caught in a magical sleep."

"For how long?" he asked, his voice more urgent now.

I took a deep breath, then said, "You've been hidden below Troll Mountain for a hundred and fifty years."

"That can't be!" He struggled to sit up but couldn't, his body weak from long disuse. "My mother! My father! What has happened to them?"

"Long gone," I said.

He uttered a deep moan. "I am starting to remember. Oh, our last words were harsh ones, and now they can never be taken back! Oh, Mother. Oh, Father!"

"Harsh in what way?" I asked.

"My parents and I had a terrible fight."

"Over what?"

"Over you. After my argument with them, I stormed out of the castle to look for you, to apologize for how I had acted when you revealed the truth to me. There was a lot to be angry about, given your falseness. But there was also the fact of your brave truth, and what I suspected it must have cost you. I wanted to see if we could be friends." He paused, put his hand on my cheek again, and said, "I have never forgotten that you had the courage to tell me the truth."

THE FATE OF THE PRINCE

From *The Annals of Troll Mountain*
By Aspen Markonnis

Using ravens and cats, word was sent throughout the mountain that the king had fled and the queen was calling a Haudglazzim in the Great Cavern.

It was the first such gathering in many years, for the king had stopped caring about the proper proceedings long ago.

As the scribe of Troll Mountain, I took my place in the niche reserved for me, from which I could observe and record all that happened. As I watched the cavern fill, I thought happily of the few moments I had been able to share with Nettie before events caught us up again.

However, I was also growing nervous. What was to be done now? Troll Mountain did need a king . . . or at least someone to be in charge of things. King Wergis had expected to live for many years to come, and in his mis-begotten pride had trained no one to take his place.

I had read enough of the outside world to know what kind of chaos was likely to come upon us if we remained leaderless. But I also knew that we did not need another tyrant.

And then there was the problem of the prince. Nettie

had woken him. But his parents, friends, family were all long gone. And Finland in the human world, his world, had no need for a prince in these modern times.

When the gathering of trolls and tonttus and ravens and cats was complete, and the cavern had been sung into a low but lasting light so that the Haudglazzim could commence, the queen stood upon the speaking stone and told everyone what had happened.

I have drawn that moment, because it was such an awesome sight.

The gathering roared in approval when they heard that the king was gone . . . and laughed uproariously at the story of the rosy fart that had sent him out of the mountain.

When they had settled, the queen said, "But now we need a new ruler."

"No king! No king!" chanted the crowd, for all had grown bitter and restless under the tyranny of Wergis.

"I will think on this," said the queen. "I will meet with my council of trolls and tonttus. Tomorrow night we will gather again to hear my suggestion. For now, go peaceful to your homes and know that the tyrant is gone and the threat to Troll Mountain is over. What will come tomorrow, we do not know. What we do know is that the long nightmare has ended."

I heard some sighs, some murmurs, a few grumbles. Even so, the cavern slowly emptied.

✦   ✦   ✦

Later that night the seven most important trolls and the five most important tonttus (myself among them) came to the queen's chambers.

Already present were Princess Nettie, Prince Gustav Fredrik, Raimo Takala and his raven, and Raimo's mostly human grandson, along with the cat and the brownie the boy had brought along on his journey.

The discussion about how to replace the king was hot

and heavy. After much back-and-forth, I suggested, "If no king, what about a mayor?"

Then I had to explain what that was.

When I was done, almost everyone agreed it was a good idea.

"But who will do it?" asked the queen. "There is no one here who has any idea how to run things."

"Actually, there is one among us who was born to rule," I said.

"Being born to rule is an outmoded idea," said Raimo.

Though I was slightly miffed by this, I took a few breaths, then said, "I agree. Let me repeat myself in a slightly different way. There is one among us who was *raised* to rule, and trained in the ways of leadership."

"Who?" asked several tonttus all at once.

"Prince Gustav Fredrik, of course."

Not surprisingly, this was greeted by cries of rage. "We will not be ruled by a human!" shouted voices from all over the cave.

"I am not talking about ruling. I am talking about leading!" I replied angrily.

That was no good, of course. I had lost the argument by getting angry. It was probably too hard to explain right then, anyway.

But the queen stepped forward and startled everyone by saying, "There is no reason that the prince must remain a human."

This was met by stunned silence, except from the prince himself, who said, "What do you mean, Hekthema?"

"You have no place in the outside world, Gustav Fredrik. That is my fault, and I apologize. And you are needed here. Which is all to the good, since you need a place to be needed. All you need do now is agree to one thing."

"And what is that?"

"How would you like to become a troll?"

The eruption of voices that followed was silenced by Hekthema roaring, "QUIET!"

Few there are who could have stilled that uproar, but she managed it.

When silence had returned, she said, "Am I not still the Witch Queen of Troll Mountain?"

After a moment of silence someone cried, "All hail the queen!"

Other voices joined in, until the cave rang with her praise.

She raised her arms.

"I will not remain queen for long if the prince agrees to my proposal." Turning to him, she said, "What shall it be, Gustav Fredrik? Will you return to the human world, where you will be a man out of place and out of time? Or will you remain with us, become one of us, and help us in our hour of need? I know you have been treated badly by us. No. I take that back. You were treated badly by *me*. But everything is changing. We are changing. You are changing. Will you change yourself to join us?"

The prince looked at Nettie and smiled. Then he turned to her mother and said, "Can you really make me a troll?"

Hekthema shook her head. "Not totally. But close enough for government work."

He nodded and replied, "Then let's do it."

The queen's face grew serious. "We need the agreement of one more person," she said.

"And that would be?" asked the prince.

"My daughter." The queen turned to Nettie. "Through my bad acts you once gained and lost this prince. Now he stands before you, ready to enter our world. Will you give up some of your trollishness to let him do so?"

Nettie did not hesitate. Looking at her mother, she said, "Tell me what I must do."

Nettie, afterward (continued)

My old friend Aspen says I did not hesitate to agree to my mother's proposal, and that is true.

But my thoughts were far from calm. What did this mean? What did it mean for me? What did it mean for the prince?

In front of all who were gathered, Mother said, "Daughter, in summoning Gustav Fredrik back from near death with your tears, you bonded with him in a very deep way. Now we must make that a bond of the body as well as the heart. Therefore, we must apply for Early Enrollment. However, we can do this only if you are completely ready for it."

"What must I do?" I asked.

Mother's face grew stern. "That is not the question, Nettie. The question is, are you truly willing? If you have doubts, this will not work. If you have qualms, it will not work. So I must ask: Are you ready to give yourself over to this?"

I looked at the prince.

I searched my heart.

Then I nodded and said, "I am ready."

Mother turned to Gustav Fredrik and asked, "Are you ready to change?"

He bowed slightly and said, "I have already changed in more ways than I have yet begun to understand. But I am ready for more."

"Then come with me," said Mother.

Turning to the others in the cave, she proclaimed, "This will take time. Tomorrow we will gather once more to see if the Entrollment is successful."

When all but our closest friends were gone, Mother turned to the prince and me and said, "This is going to hurt. But it is also everything you have wanted."

NOT WHAT I EXPECTED

From *The Memoirs of Prince Gustav Fredrik*

After what happened that night, I would say that I was the happiest of all men, save that I was no longer a man. Nor was I a troll.

I do not think there is really a word for what I had become. A truman? A humoll?

I was simply something in between.

But that was how I had felt all my life, anyway . . . something in between.

Well, that is neither here nor there. Better to talk about what actually happened.

Hekthema led Nettie and me to a small, dark place.

"This will take time," she said. "And it will not be without pain. But that is the price of transformation. I ask one last time, because this must be done without question or qualm, are you ready for this?"

I looked at Nettie. Despite her initial false front, she was the only person . . . only *being*, I suppose . . . who had ever been fully honest with me.

And all I had ever wanted was the truth.

I thought about the world I would leave behind and felt

a pang of loss. Yet I did not mourn for it. I had grown weary of its falseness. Besides, it was gone anyway, that world I had known. Had I tried to go back, I would have been entering a world as strange and unknown to me as the world of Troll Mountain.

"I am ready," I said.

Then I looked at Nettie. She was huge and hideous, but also the most honest and loving being I had ever known.

And, in truth, not entirely hideous. Her eyes were deep and wide and filled with warmth. Anyone with an ounce of sense could see that they were those of someone with a loving spirit. *That* was my Nettie, the troll girl whose tears had snatched me from the jaws of death, and worse. (And who knew until then that there really was a fate worse than death?)

"I am ready," she whispered. As she did, she looked directly into my eyes, searching for any quail or qualm.

I hope she did not see any.

"Then we begin," said Hekthema.

She rolled two boulders across the floor until they were side by side, then bade Nettie and me to sit upon them, facing each other.

When we were in position, Hekthema bared our arms. Then she pulled from her waistband a knife of stone. With it she made certain cuts in the underside of our arms.

I tried not to cry out, but I fear I made sounds that were less than brave.

Next she positioned our bare and bleeding arms, placing my right forearm palm up, Nettie's left forearm palm down against it. She did the reverse for our other arms . . . this time Nettie's below, mine on top. Once she was satisfied, she used leather thongs to bind them together.

That accomplished, she murmured some strange words.

Then she left us in the darkness for what would be the longest night of my life.

Well, the longest night was the endless night I wandered in that Enchanted Sleep. But then I was aware of nothing, merely lost in dreams, some delightful, some filled with terror.

For *this* night I was fully alert, with all my nerves on edge.

Sometimes I screamed.

The body does not change without some pain.

Nettie whimpered but did not scream. I do not know, even now, if that was because she is stronger than I am (that would not surprise me) or only because it hurts more to get larger than it does to get smaller.

I slept sometimes, I think.

Other times, Nettie and I talked. In the dark, it didn't matter what we looked like. In the dark, only truth mattered.

This was what my heart had longed for.

I had met so many princesses, so very many princesses who shimmered with beauty on the outside but spoke from places that I knew to be false.

Now my heart felt safe, and close, and at ease.

Loving and wanting are not the same thing.

Want is for taking.

Love is for giving.

And for forgiving.

I had never before felt love the way I felt it that long, painful, terrifying, and utterly beautiful night.

There were times when my body twisted in agony.

There were times when I felt swept away by bliss.

The night seemed endless ... yet when Hekthema returned to free us from our bonds, it felt as if it had been far too brief.

Nettie, afterward (continued)

I never believed I could be happy.

I never believed I could find love.

Yet here I am, happy and in love with my slightly hideous prince.

We are the same height.

I am shorter than I was. He is taller.

My teeth are straighter, his are more scraggled.

My nose is smaller, his is larger, like a half a pickle.

We look like we belong together.

He is the mayor of Troll Mountain. Someday it is likely I will be mayoress. We will take turns, when my people are ready for female leadership.

I think it will be soon.

And, who knows, the day may come when someone else is elected and we will give over our responsibilities.

That will be all right, too.

I want to do my part and make things better here in the mountain.

But I don't particularly want to be in charge of anything.

I simply want to be with the man I love.

Even if he is now half troll.

Like me.

Text messages between Raimo Takala and Cody Takala

Raimo

Thanks for the ride home, Grandson. My first time traveling in the family cauldron!

Cody

Glad to be of service, Gramps! I just wish I still had that time peg. Then I could come visit you again.

Raimo

Maybe we can arrange a somewhat more normal visit next summer.

Cody

I'd love that! But, um . . . what if Dad wants to come along?

Raimo

Well, now that Hekthema owes us a favor, I suspect she could help me look my age—my human age—for a while, so as not to upset your dad too much.

Cody

Let's plan on it!

Alex

I can't believe you sent Angus back to me via FedEx Overnight!

Cody

He was eager to get home.

Alex

Well, he changed his mind somewhere along the way. He was fit to be tied when he came out of that box.

Cody

I can just imagine!

Alex

But once he calmed down he told me everything that happened. I am boggled!

Cody

I am exhausted. But really happy.

Alex

You should be. Both.

Cody

Thank goodness the time peg worked! But I'm really going to miss Nettie. And Dad is going to be upset that he's lost one of his best workers.

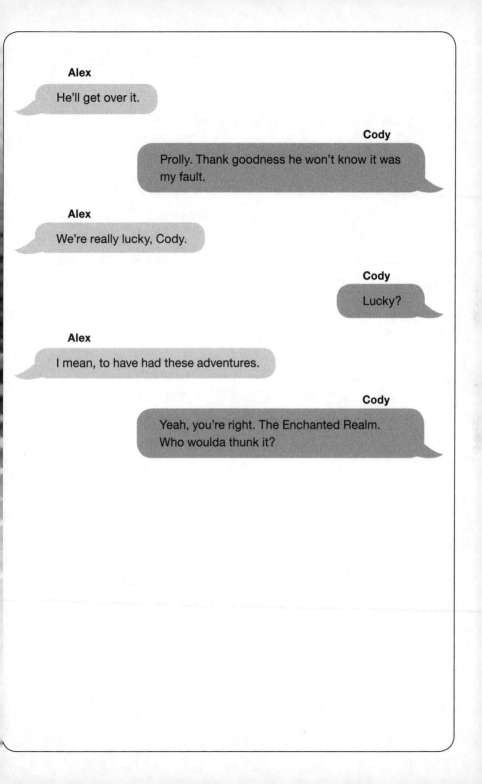

From: C-Tak@kid2kid.com
To: R.Takala@finnet.fn
Date: 12/14
Subject: THANK YOU!

Grampa,

 I got the package! Thank you. Thank you! Those pages from Nettie and Aspen and the prince are exactly what I needed to finish putting together the story of this adventure. I'll send you a copy as soon as I'm done!

Love,

Cody

SECOND AUTOBIOGRAPHY

END OF SCHOOL YEAR

My life story up to the point where I wrote it last fall is the same as it ever was, of course. (Seriously, why would it be different? Honestly, Mr. Liebe.)

Even so, I have to admit that I do understand it better. Which I guess was kind of the point.

And this year . . . oh, man, this year brought a lot of changes. And, to be truthful, most of them were spurred by this Biography Project.

I for sure learned more about my family, and myself, than I could have imagined when you assigned that first autobiography. In fact, I am now connected to my grandfather in Finland in a way that never would have happened without the project. So I need to thank you for that.

Also, I have figured out what I want to do when I grow up, which is great.

You may remember that in my first bio I said I kind of wanted to be a hero. Well, now I am, at least in a way. Close enough for me to be comfortable with that.

Unfortunately, I can't talk about it.

Let's just say it was a gas!

(I know you will think I am "skying" when I say that, but honest to roses it's absolutely true.)

And that thing about how I thought I might want to be a veterinarian? I'm totally set on that now, partly because I know I'll have help like almost no one can imagine. Cats are amazing.

I want to be the greatest vet since Dr. Dolittle.

And I am not skying when I say that!

ABOUT THE AUTHOR

BRUCE COVILLE is the author of over 100 books for children and young adults, including the international bestseller *My Teacher Is an Alien* and the wildly popular Unicorn Chronicles series. His work has appeared in more than a dozen languages and won children's choice awards in more than a dozen states. He has been, at various times, a teacher, a toy maker, a magazine editor, and a gravedigger. He is also the founder of Full Cast Audio, an audiobook publishing company devoted to producing full cast, unabridged recordings of material for family listening. Mr. Coville lives in Syracuse, New York, with his wife, author and illustrator Katherine Coville. Visit him at brucecoville.com and TheEnchantedFiles.com.

ABOUT THE ILLUSTRATOR

PAUL KIDBY is a self-taught artist whose first job was making false teeth. He eventually left the tooth business and became an illustrator. His work has appeared on computer game packaging, magazine covers, and bestselling books. Paul also enjoys sculpting, and his limited-edition bronzes are collected worldwide. Paul lives and works at his home studio in the south of England with his wife, Vanessa, and two dogs. When he is not painting, drawing, or sculpting, he is mostly found growing vegetables in his garden or walking in the countryside. Visit Paul at paulkidby.com.